The Mysterious Madness of Mormons

When religious indoctrination clashes with reality, the outcome can't always be predicted. In these stories by the author of *Please Evacuate* and *Inferno in the French Quarter*, a Seminary teacher threatens to kill his students. A schizophrenic woman in a hurricane evacuation shelter finds love. A Relief Society president's silicone breast implants develop into a new life form.

A sister missionary suffocating under family pressure is held hostage during a bank robbery. A teenage girl is haunted by the ghost of Emma Smith. A devout Mormon takes up sex work to raise money to help the poor.

Sometimes, behavior that seems perfectly reasonable in one culture can seem disturbing to those outside it. But whether reasonable or disturbing, their stories can also make compelling reading.

Praise for Johnny Townsend

In *Zombies for Jesus*, "Townsend isn't writing satire, but deeply emotional and revealing portraits of people who are, with a few exceptions, quite lovable."

Kel Munger, *Sacramento News and Review*

In *Sex among the Saints,* "Townsend writes with a deadpan wit and a supple, realistic prose that's full of psychological empathy….he takes his protagonists' moral struggles seriously and invests them with real emotional resonance."

Kirkus Reviews

Inferno in the French Quarter: The UpStairs Lounge Fire is "a gripping account of all the horrors that transpired that night, as well as a respectful remembrance of the victims."

Terry Firma, Patheos

"Johnny Townsend's 'Partying with St. Roch' [in the anthology *Latter-Gay Saints*] tells a beautiful, haunting tale."

Kent Brintnall, Out in Print: Queer Book Reviews

Selling the City of Enoch is "sharply intelligent...pleasingly complex...The stories are full of...doubters, but there's no vindictiveness in these pages; the characters continuously poke holes in Mormonism's more extravagant absurdities, but they take very little pleasure in doing so....Many of Townsend's stories...have a provocative edge to them, but this [book] displays a great deal of insight as well...a playful, biting and surprisingly warm collection."

Kirkus Reviews

Gayrabian Nights is "an allegorical tour de force...a hard-core emotional punch."

Gay. Guy. Reading and Friends

The Washing of Brains has "A lovely writing style, and each story [is] full of unique, engaging characters....immensely entertaining."

Rainbow Awards

In *Dead Mankind Walking*, "Townsend writes in an energetic prose that balances crankiness and humor....A rambunctious volume of short, well-crafted essays..."

Kirkus Reviews

The Mysterious Madness of Mormons

Johnny Townsend

Contents

The Pledge

"An inability to feel the Spirit, or a general feeling of apathy or numbness, is often a symptom of mental illness," Radisson's father read from the lds.org website. "If you really don't think you've ever felt the Spirit, son, I'm willing to pay for psychiatric help." He placed his laptop on the small table next to his easy chair.

"No, no," said Radisson. "I lied. I've felt the Spirit."

Radisson's father smiled. "I thought so. Now you need to see that you don't deny the witness of the Holy Ghost." He picked up a sheet of paper and showed it to Radisson and his brothers. "Here's a pledge I want you all to sign."

Radisson's father walked over and set the paper down on the hot chocolate table—he refused to call it a coffee table—and Radisson leaned over to read it first. At seventeen, he was just finishing his senior year of high school in Scranton. He wouldn't turn eighteen until August, so he'd have a few months of freedom before he had to leave on his mission.

He didn't particularly want to go, but there'd be no way to get out of it gracefully. Radisson had been putting money away from his summer job the past couple of years making pizzas. The problem, of course, was that the money was no longer his. Radisson's father had forced him to hand all the money over to him to put in Radisson's mission savings fund. His father was the sole owner on the account.

"It's still yours, of course," his father had explained.

The letter in front of Radisson was pretty much what he was expecting. "My love is unconditional," it began, "but my money is not." Radisson's father was always saying things like, "My love is unconditional, but my patience is not" or "My love is unconditional, but my television is not." He always raised his right hand solemnly as he spoke in case angels were recording the declaration.

Radisson wasn't sure if his father felt any love toward him at all, conditional or otherwise. He remembered the time a few years earlier when he joked at the dinner table that he must have been named after the hotel room where he'd been conceived. His father had grounded him for two weeks. But their unease with one another had begun years earlier.

Radisson couldn't pinpoint the exact beginning of the problem. His earliest memory was of his father spanking him for making too much noise during Sacrament meeting. "You have to be quiet to feel the Spirit!" his father had shouted. He couldn't have been more than four at the time.

Radisson felt his two younger brothers fidgeting on the sofa beside him, so he tried to hurry up with the letter.

"If you're going to be a Lamen or a Lemule, you will get nothing from me."

Sheesh, Dad, Radisson thought, you've read the Book of Mormon twenty times. Can't you even remember how to spell the names?

He thought about his father always saying smart alecks didn't feel the Spirit.

"If you don't complete a successful mission," the letter went on, "you won't receive any college tuition from me."

Radisson had already assumed as much. He had no idea why his father felt the need to state the obvious. Radisson should just go ahead and pass the letter on to his brothers, but he was afraid his father would give him a pop quiz before the family council was over.

"If you don't marry in the temple within two years of returning, I'll cut off tuition for the rest of your degree."

Radisson looked up at his father, who was sitting serenely in his easy chair again, a small smile on his lips. Radisson didn't want to get married at all, much less before he finished school. He'd long since decided that beating off was better than being tied down with children. He'd had enough of babysitting for his brothers over the years.

They were good kids, but he had no desire to add another eighteen years to the tally he'd already racked up. He'd simply have to get good grades those first two years to be able to get a scholarship for the rest. Too bad he'd been lazy in high school. He had several B's in addition to his A's. Even one C. That wouldn't do anymore.

"Your degree will need to be earned at BYU."

Shit!

Things were getting unreasonable. Radisson wondered if he'd be able to survive even the first two years of tuition. The last place he wanted to go to school was Brigham Young. He wanted an agricultural degree, and the Y wasn't the best place for that. He might just have to tough it out with student loans right from the beginning. Radisson's father was grossly overweight and on heart medication. At some point in the relatively near future, Radisson would be able to pay back his loans. Not a nice thing to think about, but one didn't need the Spirit to recognize facts.

"You will always keep a current temple recommend," the letter continued, "and you'll need to attend church weekly. You must prove you're reading your scriptures daily, that you pay a full tithe, and that you always keep the Word of Wisdom."

Really, Dad, the temple recommend already covers attendance and tithing and the Word of Wisdom. You're being as redundant as those Isaiah passages in 2 Nephi. And Mosiah. And 3 Nephi.

He was glad he'd never told the bishop he'd had a beer once with a friend.

But was that beer the reason he never felt the Spirit? Was the fact that he didn't become an Eagle Scout the reason? Was it hiding Pop-Tarts in his room on Fast Sunday?

"You must hold responsible callings in the Church, and you must always magnify your calling."

Just how in the world was Radisson's father going to assess *that*, he wondered? He remembered his father complaining that some of the ward members weren't scrubbing the toilets hard enough on their day to clean the meetinghouse bathrooms. Radisson had joked with his friends that CTR didn't really mean Choose the Right. It meant Clean the Restrooms.

After that first joke, when he and his best bud Heber blessed the sacrament together, they'd text each other during the rest of the meeting. Chant the Refrain one of them might text. Cool the Reactor the other would text back. Call the Repairman. Cultivate the Radishes. Create the Religion. Cum Then Repent.

When his father had gone through Radisson's cell phone and seen the texts, he'd confiscated the phone and never returned it.

"If you fail on even *one* of these requirements, you will be permanently written out of my will. No help with tuition. No help with a down payment on a house. No inheritance."

Radisson's mouth fell open. Did his father really just say that? He understood that legally, and probably morally, too, the man had no obligation to help his children financially once they reached eighteen, no matter what the conditions.

He *knew* that. He'd thought about it himself when contemplating marriage, and he'd decided that even eighteen years was too much to take on. But something about his father's declaration seemed rather…mean.

Did respect for one's father need to be unconditional?

"If you go through the motions and obey all the commandments but even *try* to persuade anyone else— family member or Church member or non-member—that the Church isn't true, you will be written out of my will."

Radisson wasn't thinking anything at all by this point, too numb to react. Since he wasn't speaking, he reflected, he couldn't really be speechless. Was he then just "thoughtless," like his father told him almost daily?

Wait, that was a thought, wasn't it?

Radisson remembered all the years he'd spent in scouting, though he hated camping. His father kept saying, "You want to be a farmer, but you don't like the outdoors?"

As if sleeping in the woods was the same thing as growing soybeans or beets. Radisson thought of the misery early morning Seminary was in his life. He thought of all the times he'd hidden carrots and other vegetables in the bathroom on a Saturday night, and then on Sunday morning gone in and chewed them up, spitting them out on the rim of the toilet bowl and spreading some around his lips, then calling his mother to say he'd vomited and couldn't go to church that day.

Was that normal teen behavior, he wondered? Maybe he *did* need to see a shrink. Maybe he did legitimately have a mental problem preventing him from feeling the Spirit. If so, his irreverence might not really be his fault. But how could he lead the religious life his father wanted him to, if he was mentally ill? It was like asking a person with Down syndrome to learn calculus.

He thought about how his father eventually started forcing him to skip Saturday night's supper so he'd never have to miss church again.

Well, he wasn't thoughtless now, was he?

"If it turns out none of you are worthy, I'll leave all my money to the Church."

The letter ended with a decree that everyone in the family sign and date it. Radisson wasn't sure a binding document could be signed by a minor, but then, this wasn't a legal contract, only a declaration of intent. He passed the note to his two brothers. Then he looked at his mother. She'd apparently have to sign the damn thing, too, or be left on her own when his father died of a heart attack.

But he wondered now if she was really the sterling member she always appeared to be, or if she was just being bullied every day like the rest of them. He couldn't read her face.

Weren't mothers supposed to protect their kids, and not just themselves?

Radisson heard Gerard, who was fourteen, murmuring as he read. "No problem, Dad. Of course. No problem, Dad." Merritt, almost twelve, said nothing. But he looked at Radisson, and when their eyes locked, Radisson *knew*. He felt a shiver down his spine.

Was that the Spirit?

"Wow, Dad," he said in the cheeriest voice he could muster. "That's a great lesson. You made your point better than anything I've ever heard in church." It was a long shot, but it was the only one he had. Maybe now that he was finally in tune, the Spirit was telling him what to say.

If he was listening to the *right* Spirit.

Radisson's father frowned.

"We're always taught about the War in Heaven," Radisson went on. "How Lucifer wanted to force everyone to be obedient but Jesus wanted to give people their free agency."

"That's right," said his father. "That's exactly right."

"Your fake letter is a perfect example of what life would have been like had Heavenly Father accepted Lucifer's plan."

The room went deathly quiet. Radisson could feel his brothers' eyes boring into him. He could hear his own breathing. His mother stared at the floor. "Young man," Radisson's father said coolly, "your humor is sorely lacking. As always."

"You mean the letter's real?"

"You know damn well it is," Radisson's father spit out. "And this letter is all about agency. But free agency never meant there wouldn't be consequences for your actions." He set a pen down on the hot chocolate table. Radisson noticed it was a gel pen. The kind with ink you couldn't erase.

"As the oldest son," Radisson's father intoned, "I think you should sign it first." He pointed to the pen.

Radisson picked it up and reached for the letter. He turned to his mother, looking at him again with that inscrutable face, her gaze seeming to focus on a spot somewhere behind him. He looked at Gerard, smiling encouragingly. And he looked at Merritt.

Then he signed. Radisson's father smiled, but Radisson felt no warmth. He strained to see if expressions like that had the ability to create any smile lines in his father's face.

"Dad," said Gerard, "Radisson signed his name 'Korihor.'"

Radisson's father leaped out of his chair and snatched the paper from Gerard's hands. "You little…you little…"

"Joseph Smith III?" Radisson suggested.

His father's face turned red. But there was no way to win, Radisson realized. His father held all the power.

This must be what Spirit Prison was like, he thought. Then he wondered if the Spirit could even work in prison. Maybe there was a reason he'd never felt its influence.

"Dad, I think I'm going to take you up on your offer," he said. His father glowered. "I want to see a psychiatrist." He paused. "*Not* one from the Church." Since they lived in Pennsylvania, there was a good chance of finding a secular doctor in any case. He probably shouldn't have specified.

Radisson watched as Gerard and then Merritt signed the pledge.

"All right, son," Radisson's father said in a voice that sucked all warmth from the room. "But you're under strict curfew from now until you turn eighteen. And if you haven't repented by then…"

"I'll be cast out of heaven?"

Radisson thought his father might hit him. He wondered for a brief second if he'd be able to get his father angry enough to have a heart attack before he could rewrite his will, but then he realized such a thought only proved he was completely and utterly cut off from the Holy Ghost. He stood and walked to the room he shared with Gerard. If only he had a computer, he thought. If only he had a phone like normal kids.

But he wasn't normal. He was spiritually deaf. Spiritually blind.

He sat at his desk and picked up his Book of Mormon, thumbing through the index. It was like feeling pages full of Braille in front of him while having no understanding of the dots. He had no choice but to listen to the *other* Spirit. He opened to a section on the Mulekites and began writing down all the reasons their story made no sense.

Taking Off the Mask

Mallory sat in the chair, completely motionless. Her hands were gloved, and she was wearing a rubber mask featuring a generic female vampire's face. Through the openings in the mask, she watched as three young children scampered along the sidewalk in front of her frame shop in West Jordan.

One of the boys, perhaps eight years old, stopped to look in at the display: a vampire holding a book titled *Effective Sunblock Techniques*.

The boy studied the display, the plastic spiders and fake webs, the goblets with lizard tails hanging over the edges. But then he looked more closely at Mallory, squinting. He carefully looked her up and down and was just about to call to one of his siblings when Mallory quickly turned a page in the book and then froze again.

The boy's eyes widened and he pressed his face against the glass. Mallory remained completely motionless, not even blinking. The boy called out for his siblings, who came over to peer through the window as well. One was a girl about seven and the other a boy perhaps five years old. Mallory didn't move a muscle.

Then she heard the older child calling out to his parents somewhere beyond her line of sight. While all three children watched, she turned another page. They all started shouting for their parents to hurry up.

When the parents reached the window, Mallory heard the kids insisting the vampire was real. The parents smiled good-naturedly and started to move off, but the older boy tugged on his mother's arm. "No, Mom, it's true. It's true. You have to believe me. There's a person behind that mask."

He finally succeeded in getting the parents to look one last time through the window at the display. At that point, Mallory suddenly jumped up toward the glass and screamed like she'd been stabbed, and all five members of the family screamed as well. Then the parents started laughing, and Mallory waved pleasantly at them before they pulled the kids away. The father had been rather good looking.

Mallory sat in the window another forty-five minutes, pulling the same stunt on two more families that walked through the strip mall. She loved Halloween, such a fun time to play with children.

Not that she wanted any of her own. Even now, she liked teasing them more than interacting with them on a more human level. Mallory had enjoyed being a kid well enough, playing with her brothers and sisters and cousins. But now she had little use for what she called "miniature humans." She had no plans to give out treats the following evening when the neighborhood kids went door to door. She could barely tolerate her time each Sunday in the Nursery at church.

Someday, maybe, she'd volunteer as a Big Sister downtown, but that time wasn't now. Greg kept asking when they could start trying to get pregnant, but Mallory insisted on keeping her diaphragm firmly in place. "It's great that you love your job," Greg said, "but your main job is to be a wife and mother."

"When you're ready to carry the baby for nine months," Mallory would reply, "we can talk."

It was almost 7:00, two hours past closing time, and Greg would be starving. There were only a few days of the year when she could really play, though, and she wasn't going to throw them away. She climbed into her car, still dressed as a vampire, and started home. At a stoplight, she noticed a well-dressed woman in the car next to hers cast a disapproving look as Mallory sang along to Pink's "Raise Your Glass" while still in her mask.

It wasn't safe to drive with her vision restricted, but who always wanted to be safe? She stopped at Subway to pick up two foot-long sandwiches, vegetarian for her and pulled pork for Greg. She'd have a V-8 from the fridge at home to stay in character, she decided.

"How's my darling bloodsucker?" Greg asked as Mallory walked through the door.

"In the mood to suck," she replied, setting the food on the table. She pulled off her mask and then kneeled in front of her husband.

"Can't it wait?" he asked, reaching over her head to start unwrapping one of the sandwiches. "This one's yours," he said.

Mallory stood back up and went to grab her V-8 and a can of Sprite for Greg. During dinner, Greg talked about his day at the office, and Mallory described a custom frame job she was doing, an entire family dressed as fairies, even the father. Mallory was doing some special stenciling and decorating with the mats. Neither she nor Greg seemed very interested in the other's day. *If I cared about office work,* Mallory thought, *I'd have a job in an office.* She supposed he felt the same way about mats and frames.

"Why don't you get a costume for tomorrow night?" asked Mallory. "We could have our own little Halloween party with the lights on low so no kids knock on the door."

"The Church disapproves of members wearing masks," he replied.

Then can I put a bag over your head? Mallory wanted to ask. Really, Greg was attractive enough, but sometimes she grew tired of looking at him. Couldn't he loosen up just one night of the year? He never wore costumes for Halloween and didn't even like getting dressed up when they went to the symphony. She wanted some role play, have Greg pretend to be the bishop or a visiting General Authority, but she was lucky sometimes if she could just get him hard.

After dinner, they moved to the sofa to watch an episode of *Supergirl*. Mallory tried going down on Greg again, but he fell asleep before she could finish. Greg routinely seemed less than enthused about sex. Mallory, on the other hand, could hardly get enough. She didn't particularly want intercourse or to have an orgasm herself. She simply enjoyed taking a penis in her mouth.

In fact, she enjoyed it a great deal more than Greg appeared to enjoy being attended to. It was too bad the days of Joseph Smith's polyandry were over. Mallory could see herself sucking a different dick every day of the week, perhaps saving intercourse solely for Sunday afternoons.

Mallory quietly removed herself from the sofa, leaving her dozing husband and heading to the home office. Greg used it more than she did, but she was free to use it when Greg wasn't around. She navigated to Craigslist and went to the personals. Men Seeking Women.

Most of the ads were complete turn-offs. Men simply did not know how to approach women. She wondered if it was just as bad outside of Salt Lake. Perhaps Mormon men were never taught how to interact properly with grown women.

She turned the radio on to try to distract herself. David Guetta was singing "Titanium."

Mallory moved to Women Seeking Men and hesitated. She'd never cheated on Greg and had been a virgin when they married four years ago. But she didn't think she could face a lifetime of a limp dick dozing on the sofa. She nodded and then composed her own ad.

It was just an exercise, of course. She didn't expect anyone to respond, and if they did, she wouldn't write back. Just to make sure she didn't receive many hits, though, she added a closing line to her ad: Men with current temple recommends given preference.

That should scare away pretty much everybody.

Mallory walked back to the living room and looked longingly at Greg's still exposed penis. She really did wish polyandry would come back. There was no way to get a letter to the Prophet, unfortunately, but maybe she could have a letter to the editor published in the *Deseret News.*

Long after their show was over and Mallory was watching Fox news, Greg stirred. "Mmm, how long have I been out?" He looked at his penis as if not recognizing what it was.

Mallory wished that she could come out.

"I want some dessert," she said, pointing.

Greg grinned and started fondling himself until he became half erect. Then he turned up his hands and shrugged. "Too tired," he said. "I promise I'll be in the mood tomorrow." He gave her a kiss and then headed to the bedroom.

It was only 9:40, and Mallory didn't open her shop until 10:00 the next morning. She went back to the office and checked the computer. There were eleven responses to her ad. Five of them had attachments showing a redacted temple recommend.

I'll be damned, she thought. Then she realized that she probably would be. She sent emails to the five men who'd shown their recommends. Three responded within the following ten minutes.

Is it this easy? she wondered. All this time she could have been having other men in her life. Certainly, the sex was tempting, but really, she just wanted conversation with other adults, adults who didn't only talk about their kids, like the women at church, or talk only about their work, like Greg. Of course, there was no guarantee these guys would be any better, but she could put the ad up as often as necessary until she found what she needed.

Two of the men wanted to meet that night and the other the following evening. Mallory was certain she could slip out of the house without Greg noticing, but the thought made her feel a bit like a rotting Halloween pumpkin.

If her choice was either to feel slimy or feel suffocated, which was the better option? She wasn't sure she knew.

Mallory went to the bathroom to splash some water on her face. Looking at her reflection, she realized she was still wearing her vampire costume. A member of the undead. A life confined to one man or a life of deceit.

It just wouldn't do.

Mallory went to the bedroom and turned on the lamp next to Greg's pillow. "Huh? Wha?" he mumbled.

"Greg, we have to talk." She helped pull Greg to a sitting position and threw the partially filled glass of water resting next to the lamp into Greg's face.

"What the heck!"

"Greg, I love you, but I need something more. I don't want to do anything behind your back, but here's the situation." Mallory described her ad and the response to it.

"Why temple recommends?" asked Greg, appearing to be back in a daze. Mallory wasn't sure he was fully awake yet. But then, he always seemed to go through life half asleep. That was part of the problem.

"I wanted men who shared my values." She was silent a long moment, waiting for Greg to say something. He didn't. "So, Greg," she said finally, "I think I'm going to invite one of the men over. We can use the spare bedroom."

Greg held up a hand. "Wait a second. Wait a second." He paused, and Mallory waited, but he didn't go on. Finally, she took a breath and was about to speak again when he continued. "I want other men in my life, too," he said. "You want polyandry. I just want at least one man. I know I should have told you this before, but…"

"You're gay?" she asked, nodding slowly. "That explains a lot."

"No, I'm bisexual," he clarified. "I really am interested in you. But when it's *only* you…"

Mallory thought it would be inappropriate to feel offended after everything she'd just revealed to Greg. So she forced a smile instead.

"I can write back to these guys and ask if they're interested in a three-way," Mallory offered. "If they're not, I can write a new ad tomorrow."

Greg smiled back at her. His looked genuine. Then he pointed with both fingers at his crotch. "Hey," he said, "I think I'm feeling something down there."

Bully for you, Mallory thought. She stood up and headed to the bedroom door. Then she paused and turned back. "A three-way is fine for now," she said. "Maybe even two or three three-ways a week. But…"

"Yes?"

"Do you think you'd be up for real polyandry sometime? We could look together for a permanent third partner." And maybe eventually a fourth?

"You'd better go back to the computer," said Greg. "If you keep talking like that, I'll be done before anyone comes over at all."

Could that hurdle have been cleared so easily, too? Mallory felt as if someone had just pulled a stake from her heart. Why in the world did people live decades of their lives in misery when sometimes simply saying what was on your mind could change everything?

Because change killed one thing while bringing another to life?

Mallory quickly sent off a couple of emails, and there was one response within another five minutes. "I'm okay with a three-way tonight," said the man. "But I have to see your temple recommends first. Turnabout is fair play. And I'm hoping for a lot of turnabout tonight."

Mallory took pictures of hers and Greg's temple recommends and sent them back. It wasn't until she hit Send that she realized she'd forgotten to redact them. Five minutes later, another email showed up in her inbox. "Hi, Mallory, it's your cousin, Spencer." Mallory knew the name immediately, despite the abundance of cousins. One of her favorites, he was two years her junior and still unmarried, second counselor in his ward's Elders Quorum. "Is it still okay if I come over?"

Well, it wasn't as if they were going to have kids together. Mallory typed back Yes and included her address, just in case Spencer had forgotten it. "But do you have a costume you can wear?" she added. "Tomorrow is Halloween, and I feel like dressing up tonight."

"Will a cape and fangs do?" came the quick reply.

"We'll be waiting with the porch light on," she wrote back.

Such a fun idea, thought Mallory. And the evening might have been a disaster instead. As she looked at the light beside the front door, she decided that maybe the following evening she would leave it on as well and be ready with a bucket full of candy. She could put up with kids for one night.

"Greg," she called out toward the bedroom. "Put on your temple clothes."

"Why?"

Mallory stuck her head in the bedroom. "You're going to pretend to be the corpse we drained of blood, lying in your burial clothes about to be buried, but we'll bring you back to life *somehow*."

Greg looked at her with a blank expression for the longest time, and then he smiled. This time, Mallory's smile back was genuine, too.

The Day I Killed My Seminary Teacher

Joseph hated early morning Seminary. It wasn't that he didn't like learning about the gospel. It was just that he'd rather study on his own, without all the negativity from so many of his classmates. It seemed as if all they did every morning was argue.

Of course, attending each day did give him a chance to see Tiffany more often. They were both in eleventh grade and shared American History and English classes together at the high school, so he'd have seen her anyway, but there was something different about seeing her in a church setting.

She seemed more attractive when she was talking about Heavenly Father. Her hair was just as beautiful either way, long and golden, but at church, she had a special glow. He finally worked up the nerve to tell her so today.

"It's the Mountain Dew," she whispered. Philip, sitting at the next desk over, snickered.

Joseph's mouth fell open. Then he closed it and smiled. Tiffany was always pretending to be radical. She'd once even said she believed in gay marriage. But no one so lovely could possibly be that big a sinner.

He wondered if she'd wait two years while he was away on his mission. Someone that beautiful would be tempted not to, but someone that beautiful was also sure to be pure and faithful. How could she not be? Helen of Troy had been faithful. It wasn't her fault she was kidnapped.

Joseph stole a glance at Philip. Philip was a senior, almost old enough to serve a mission, but he'd recently grown a moustache and was rumored to drink coffee.

"Pipe down, everyone," Brother Robertson said in a stern voice. He rapped his desk with a baton. Brother Robertson had told the class at the beginning of the year that he used the baton because he was "conducting the music of gospel truth." Even Joseph had rolled his eyes at that. "Shelly, will you give the opening prayer?"

He pointed his baton at a slightly overweight fifteen-year-old with acne on her chin. She nodded nervously and lowered her head, mumbling in a voice so low Joseph wasn't sure when to say "Amen."

"This morning, we're discussing one of the most pivotal moments in Church history," said Brother Robertson, "the martyrdom at Carthage."

Philip's hand went up.

"Yes, Philip?"

"I read that the reason Joseph Smith was arrested was for destroying a newspaper printing press."

"They were about to publish lies about the Prophet," said Brother Robertson.

"I read they were going to publish something about Joseph Smith's polygamy," Philip went on.

Brother Robertson stiffened. "They were going to make it look ugly," he said. "Deceit is the same thing as lying. Besides, there is a time and a season for everything. It wasn't time for the Lord to have polygamy made public yet."

Joseph had to agree with that time and season bit. He'd loved Tiffany for over a year, but it had never been the right time to say anything. He didn't have his final growth spurt until last summer, and then he still had to wait to get his braces off. But the right time was almost here. She'd know he loved her soul as much as her golden glow before the day was over.

Tiffany raised her hand, making Joseph smile. She'd show her true colors and defend the Prophet. The time was *always* right to stand up for the Church.

"Yes, Tiffany?"

"I thought the Church said the United States was established by Heavenly Father."

"So?" asked Brother Robertson.

"So shouldn't the Church believe in the First Amendment? Freedom of the press?"

Brother Robertson sighed heavily. "A press that lies isn't promoting freedom for anyone," he said. "Can we please get back to the lesson?"

Philip raised his hand again.

"Yes, Philip?" Brother Robertson asked wearily.

"So the rules only apply to others?" he asked. "And not to us?"

Rita raised her hand but didn't wait to be called upon. She was the teacher's daughter. "That's right," she said. "It's just like Nephi killing Laban. *Normally* killing is wrong, but not when God tells you to do it."

"Excellent example, Rita." Brother Robertson winked at her. "And now back to our lesson."

"You're saying that if God asked you to murder someone, you'd do it?" Philip turned to Rita two seats over. She nodded with a tight smile on her lips.

"What if God told you to kill several people?" Tiffany asked.

"I do whatever God wants," Rita replied. "It's called obedience. You should try it sometime."

"Class…" Brother Robertson raised his baton. He looked sternly at Rita, but there still seemed to be a twinkle in his eyes. Joseph kept watching the debate with a feeling of utter confusion.

Why was Tiffany saying those things? Acting as if she didn't believe? She'd said before that she believed it was okay to wear sleeveless dresses. She'd said she believed drinking coffee was okay, but that was almost certainly because of Philip's bad influence.

He knew she was good at heart, and she'd never come out against the Church itself before. Her mother was the Relief Society president. Her brother was an assistant to the mission president in London right now. She came from a good family.

And she was so pretty.

Maybe that was the problem. Sometimes, Satan took advantage of a person's pride. Girls were especially susceptible. Joseph would have to ask her out and then call her the day before their date and say something had come up. It would be difficult to deliberately pass up an evening with such an exceptional person, but sometimes, a guy had to do the right thing to help a girl get back on the strait and narrow.

"What if God asked you to kill an entire people?" Tiffany asked. "Would you do that?"

Please, Tiffany, stop talking.

"I do whatever Heavenly Father asks of me."

Sometimes, Mormons were their own worst enemies. Even Joseph thought Rita was being a bit unreasonable. It was almost certainly wrong to kill an *entire* group of people. The rest of the students were watching the exchange like a tennis match. Philip kept giving Tiffany an annoying smile.

Then Philip spoke up again. "So it's wrong for Hitler or for terrorists, but it's okay for *you*?"

"Not just me. For anyone who follows the Prophet."

Brother Robertson tapped on his desk with the baton. He had to tap for quite a few seconds before everyone finally turned their attention to him. "You'll remember," he said, "that God told the Hebrews to kill the Philistines when they entered the Promised Land. They didn't, and now they have the Palestinians to worry about. It's always best to obey Heavenly Father."

"I thought Jesus was the God of the Old Testament," said Richard, a boy sitting right behind Rita, "not Heavenly Father." Rita turned to give him a glare, but it wasn't as strong as the glare Brother Robertson sent his way. Joseph just wanted to get back to the approved Seminary lesson. That was why they were all here, wasn't it? He should stand up and demand that the class calm down and pay Brother Robertson some respect.

If only he'd grown just one more inch last summer, he thought.

"Only *we* are led by God," said Rita, "and anything God asks *us* to do is right by definition."

Joseph vaguely remembered seeing a movie his parents had made him watch so he could write a report to earn extra credit for Civics class, about some old president who'd said something similar. "If the president does it, it isn't illegal." Or something like that.

"I read that Joseph Smith was drinking when the mob came," said Richard, "and that he was the one who started shooting."

"Lies," said Brother Robertson. "You have to consider your source."

Of course it was lies, thought Joseph. How could a prisoner have a gun? Why wouldn't everyone just shut up? He looked at Brother Robertson, willing him to be stronger so he could control the class. Please, Heavenly Father, he sent up a silent prayer. Please.

"You can find the truth on any of a hundred different websites," Tiffany went on. "It isn't my job to keep the Church's secrets. I failed my Biology test last week because I was too sleepy to concentrate. I hate Seminary." Joseph couldn't believe what he was hearing. Such a pathetic excuse. That wasn't worthy of her at all. She was killing him.

"It's not the Church's fault you stayed up too late," Brother Robertson replied, and Joseph had to agree. "No one forced you to lose sleep. That was your choice. The wicked always blame everything on others."

Please, thought Joseph, feel the Spirit. Repent. If she didn't repent, they couldn't get married in the temple.

"So now I'm wicked?" Tiffany asked.

Yes, thought Joseph. Yes, you are. He almost wasn't sure he even wanted to go out with her anymore. "Let's listen to the teacher," Joseph finally said, his voice shaking. "We're here to learn history, not talk about Biology. If we pay attention, we can at least pass our History tests."

He was almost too scared to look at Tiffany to see her reaction, but he couldn't resist. She gave a gentle smile in his direction. What a work of art. Just like the Mona Lisa. If Heavenly Father had put in that much effort, then Joseph could, too. Maybe he'd offer to help her study.

Brother Robertson finally regained control of the class and continued with the lesson. The prophet was going to escape before he was arrested, but he heard members complaining that he was a coward, so he went "like a lamb to the slaughter" to prove them wrong.

A mob attacked the jail, and Joseph Smith recognized some of the people in the crowd as Masons, so he shouted out a Masonic code to let them know *he* knew they were betraying another Mason. Then he fell dead in the courtyard after jumping from the window of the cell. "Thus, he sealed his testimony with his blood," Brother Robertson concluded.

Joseph looked at his watch. The lesson had ended a little early, with ten minutes to spare, even with all the interruptions. It might give him a little time to talk to Tiffany before their parents came to pick them up. He just had to ask her out. Canceling on her would be for her own good. Once she was humbled, she'd see that he had her best interests at heart and go out with him for real when he asked a second time.

He shook his head. Damn, it was hard to do the right thing. But then, that was why so few made it to the Celestial Kingdom. He started trying to formulate the words he was going to use.

"Do all of you think you could die for the truth?" Brother Robertson asked suddenly. Joseph turned to look at him. Was he still teaching? They hadn't had a closing prayer yet.

"I wouldn't die for the Church," said Philip. "I don't believe in it."

"But would you die for *your* truth?" Brother Robertson pressed. "Would you die to prove you believed the Church was a lie?"

Philip laughed. "You can't be a negative martyr," he said. "Only pro."

"All right," said Brother Robertson. "How about this? Are you willing at least to stand up to show what you believe?"

Philip frowned, and Joseph had to admit he didn't know where this was leading, either. He looked at Tiffany, who was turned toward Philip. He could see just enough of her face to know she was rolling her eyes.

He simply had to ask her out today.

"Class," said Brother Robertson, "I want everyone who believes the Church is true to stand on my right. And everyone who thinks they know better than we do to stand on my left." No one moved at first, and Brother Robertson tapped his baton on his desk. "Come on," he said. "Stand behind your words."

The students slowly rose from their seats. Joseph was quick to move to the teacher's right. He was followed by Rita and Shelly and Clark. Joseph was horrified to see Tiffany follow Richard, Millie, and Philip to the left. He noted that they were evenly divided.

But this wasn't something you could just cast a vote on. The Church was true whether a person believed it or not. Even the third of all those spirits in the Pre-Existence that had been cast into Outer Darkness with Satan knew the Church was true. It didn't stop being true just because you were in Hell.

Joseph needed to figure out some way a beautiful girl who didn't believe in the gospel would say yes to a dorky boy who did believe. He couldn't help her unless she said yes. His father was in the bishopric, and Joseph almost always won the scripture chases in class. That had to be reasonably tempting. And who wouldn't want to go out with an A student?

Well, A-.

"Oh my god!" Millie suddenly squealed.

Joseph frowned at the profanity. But then he looked where Millie was pointing. Brother Robertson had pulled out a gun and was waving it in the direction of the apostates. Joseph felt his heart beat faster. What was the man doing?

"We'll see if you're willing to back up your cynicism," Brother Robertson said. "Or if you're just bluffing."

"Dad," Rita said carefully. No one else said a word. Rita moved a few inches closer to her father. Brother Robertson waved her back.

"I know the only way to guarantee you people make it to the Celestial Kingdom is for you to die as martyrs." Everyone stared, wide-eyed. "You still believe *a little* or you wouldn't be here. And you're dying in church during Seminary, so in Heavenly Father's eyes, you're dying as martyrs for the truth, even if you claim you don't believe. It's for your own good." He pointed the gun at Tiffany. "Ladies first," he said.

They practiced active shooter drills at school, but this wasn't really that, was it? They *knew* Brother Robertson.

Joseph thought his heart might burst right out of his chest, it hurt so much. He looked at Tiffany, whose eyes were darting left and right as she tried to figure out what to do. Joseph *couldn't* let her die in her sins. That would just be too awful. He owed it to her to do something.

His heart about to explode, he lunged forward and grabbed a desk from the front row, lifted it over his head with a rush of adrenalin, and brought it crashing down on Brother Robertson.

Joseph heard a sickening crack when the desk struck the teacher's head, and he watched in shock as the man fell to the floor and a pool of red liquid started spreading. Joseph kicked the gun out of Brother Robertson's reach, even though the man was no longer moving.

He stared at Tiffany. He'd just saved her life. She was sure to go out with him now. He might not even have to cancel the date to bring her around.

Rita screamed and the world came back into focus.

"What have you done!?" Rita knelt beside her father. "It was a fake gun, you idiot! This was all just part of the lesson on martyrdom!" She put her hand beneath her father's head and pulled it back, covered with blood. "Oh, my heck! Oh, my heck!"

Joseph stood in a daze while Philip whipped out his cell phone and called 9-1-1. Joseph looked at Tiffany, whose face was filled with a combination of horror and disgust as she looked back at him. After Philip hung up, he took Tiffany in his arms and hugged her.

It struck Joseph that he'd just made Brother Robertson a martyr, ensured their Seminary teacher's exaltation. Not even missionaries could be sure anyone they baptized would make it to the Celestial Kingdom.

Getting at least one person there had to count for something.

Tiffany was good in English, Joseph remembered. Maybe he could get her to help him write an essay or a letter of apology to the judge ruling over his trial, help him explain how he was still a hero who'd rescued the girl he loved.

She'd eventually understand. She was just too shaken to think clearly right now. He wondered how long he'd be in jail. Even the prophets and apostles had been in jail.

He wondered if Tiffany would wait for him.

A Little Test

Oh, brother, thought Brian when he saw the post on Facebook. Not another one. David, a "friend" he had never met in person, wanted all his Facebook friends to reply with a short note detailing how they knew each other.

But more than that, each friend was asked, *ordered* really, to copy and paste—not Share—the request in their own post "so the whole Facebook community will feel united." And then came the taunt. "I bet most of you won't do it."

Brian had "met" David three years ago when he'd Liked a comment David had made on another friend's post. David had seen the Like, sent him a private message saying, "Hey, great minds think alike! Can I be your friend?"

Brian wasn't sure if David would be able to verify if he'd complied with his copy and paste command or not, and since he didn't want the man to feel he wasn't a good friend, he did as he was told.

He'd had enough of Facebook for the time being, though, and entered sltrib.com into the address bar. While he lived happily in Vancouver BC, reading the *Salt Lake Tribune* was the easiest way to keep up with the Church. He liked *Deseret News* as well, but somehow, their coverage always seemed to miss stories the *Trib* carried. He regularly read both to make sure he heard all sides of the issues facing the Church.

"Whoa," he said when he read the headline this morning. "Native American group sues LDS Church over artifacts." The article explained that the group in question considered the Golden Plates to be Indian artifacts, and if the Church's claim that the plates were real was true, then the Church had an obligation to turn them over to their rightful owners.

Brian couldn't believe his eyes. What was the world coming to? High priests playing on their cell phones all throughout Sacrament meeting. Neighbors wishing everyone Happy Holidays instead of Merry Christmas. Women wearing sleeveless dresses in their Christmas photos. And now this.

He shook his head, feeling overwhelmed by the world. It was still early on a Saturday morning, and already Brian found he had to turn off the computer. He went to the kitchen and started frying some bacon. The smell awakened his wife Lotte, and soon they were at the kitchen table eating breakfast together.

"Any special plans for the day?" Lotte asked, sipping her orange juice.

"I thought I might run over to the temple and squeeze in an endowment." He took a bite of his scrambled eggs. "You want to come?"

She'd passed on Christmas caroling last week and on selecting gifts to donate to underprivileged children a few days later. She hadn't come along last night when he'd gone to the hospital to visit Brother Farrell, who was recovering from a stroke. Brother Farrell had resigned from the Church over a year ago, but Brian still felt he deserved to have some of his old friends check in on him.

To be fair, though, Brian hadn't joined in when his wife baked snickerdoodles for the Relief Society two weeks ago.

"No. I'm meeting with the girls today." Lotte and her Relief Society friends were all in their fifties and sixties. "It's trading day." The women were voracious readers of racy romance novels and sometimes went on outings to used book stores.

The Church always warned men against the dangers of pornography, but it seemed women got a free pass. Brian had tried to read one of his wife's books to get some acceptable sexual stimulation, but he found the thing utterly boring. If only reading wasn't such a solitary activity.

Thinking about sex again got him aroused, though, so while Lotte took care of the dishes, he went to the bathroom and took care of himself. With his cum soaking the folded toilet paper in his hand, he wondered how he was going to be able to enter the temple this morning without everyone being able to tell what he'd just done. He remembered the time a couple of months ago when the bishop had started Sacrament meeting by declaring, "There's a man here today who is unworthy. We can't begin until he leaves the chapel."

After a couple of minutes of strained silence, three different men had stood and slinked out. Brian couldn't bear it if the same thing happened at the temple today. After one session where two attractive women had been part of the prayer circle, he'd beaten off in the temple bathroom and then hunkered down in the stall for almost an hour, afraid to come out and let everyone see his countenance.

Or his misdemeanor, as his wife called the look on his face whenever she caught him in the act.

Earth life was all about tests, and this was one he failed consistently. It wasn't Lotte's fault she was no longer interested in physical intimacy. Brian had never been that good at lovemaking to begin with, and with those racy novels at her fingertips now, his wife seemed to get all the satisfaction she needed.

He wondered if Lotte ever masturbated, but he couldn't honestly imagine his wife doing such a vile thing.

Brian squeezed the last drop of semen out of his penis, tossed the tissue in the toilet, and flushed. He sprayed air freshener into the air so if Lotte came into the bathroom, she'd think he'd been defecating. There was no other reason for him to have taken so long.

Brian looked at his watch and frowned. He didn't want to arrive at the temple too early. All the old people went first thing in the morning. He was only fifty-seven. He decided to sit outside on the front porch and watch the falling snow for a while before leaving. The temperature was just above freezing, so most of the snow melted as soon as it hit the pavement, though a little accumulated on the grass.

The flakes fell so gracefully that Brian was mesmerized. What with global warming, he treated every snowfall as if it might be his last. There were winters in Vancouver when there might be only one significant snowfall the entire season. The world was soon going to be robbed of this beauty.

Mankind had failed the test of stewardship. It couldn't be long before the tribulations of the Last Days began, and only a little longer before Christ returned. He could hardly wait.

But would there be snow during the Millennium, he wondered? Brian didn't know if the cold weather most people despised would be allowed during the thousand years of Christ's reign. If there was any chance of snuggling with Lotte, it was during the winter.

He hoped the Last Days wouldn't come too soon.

The door opened. "Get back in here before you catch cold," his wife ordered. "If you get sick, I get sick, and then when I volunteer at the community center, the people there get sick. I'm just not in the mood." Brian nodded and went back into the house. He logged onto an anti-fracking website and donated fifteen dollars. After tithing, there was so little left to put toward other good causes, but he felt he had to at least make an effort.

One of the wrapped gifts waiting underneath the tree was a blanket featuring the cover of Lotte's favorite romance novel, one she refused to trade with the other women. He'd had it blown up and transferred to fabric. Perhaps Lotte would like snuggling under that.

Brian changed into his gray suit, but feeling a bit adrift, he decided to check Facebook once more before he left. Ten posts in, he groaned. Not another one.

"This is a little test to see if my friends actually read my posts. If you've ever known anyone who died of cancer, you need to copy and paste this message into your own post and spread the word about the importance of research. I know my real friends will make the effort to help."

Brian considered clicking on the angry face emoji. If one of his friends wanted to write a post on the importance of cancer research, he'd be more than happy to Share it. But no, people had to command others exactly how to behave. He wasn't allowed to post an article of his own choosing on the subject or write his own thoughts. No, the friend only allowed one option on how to proceed. If he failed, he was a bad person.

He thought about all the times his mission president had forced him to bear his testimony, even when he didn't feel like it. He thought about the times he'd gone Home Teaching and had to ask his Home Teaching families if they'd done their own Home Teaching.

He thought about the times he'd played Tag as a kid.

Brian looked at the computer screen in front of him, wishing he hadn't turned it on. He couldn't afford to lose any of his social contacts, so he did what he'd been ordered to do.

He felt dirty.

A few moments later, Brian leaned down to kiss Lotte on the cheek as she sat on the sofa reading. "See you in a few hours."

"Gotta finish this before the girls get here," she replied, not even looking up from her book.

The drive to the temple took longer than usual. While there was little ice on the roads, drivers still acted as if there were. By the time he finally arrived, the snow had turned to light rain and was melting what was left.

Brian changed into his white pants and carried his pouch of accessories to the endowment room. He sat on the right with the other men. There were far more women in the room on the left side. Women always seemed to obey the commandments better than men. It was why there were going to be more women in the Celestial Kingdom. The reason polygamy was an eternal principle.

Brian wondered if Heavenly Father's mortal wife had made it to the highest degree of heaven with him, or if he got a fresh wife once he arrived. He wondered if there were conjugal visits to the lower kingdoms if one's mortal spouse didn't make it. He wondered if resurrected beings automatically had healthy sex drives.

"If any of you feel you cannot make these sacred vows today, you may stand up and leave the room."

A test to see if people were faithful enough to stay seated even though they were committing in advance to vows whose content they weren't aware of yet.

Brian was so tired of tests. He'd been tested in the Pre-Existence to see if he was worthy enough to be born into the Church. He'd been tested in this life to see if he was willing to serve a mission. He'd been tested to see if he was worthy enough to find converts. Tested to see if he'd marry in the temple, have kids, pay his tithing, avoid the evils of coffee and tea. He was tested to see if he would humble himself to scrub church toilets once a month.

He was tested to see if he could remain morally clean even when his wife's lack of participation in Celestial duties was making it difficult.

Brian watched the temple movie, watched as Adam and Eve failed their first test. And passed it by doing so.

He almost fell asleep while Lucifer was talking.

Finally, after what seemed an eternity, he passed through the veil into the Celestial Room. He'd passed the proxy test numerous times over the years yet couldn't help but worry if he'd pass the real thing.

A woman in a tight white dress wearing a tight green apron walked past. Brian closed his eyes.

He thought about what might go on in the Holy of Holies.

Brian wondered if he took Lotte's books away, if she might be more inclined to be intimate with him.

Were they *both* failing the test of an eternal marriage?

After Brian changed back into his suit, he stopped by a Thai restaurant on his way home. Lotte hated Thai food. He had to admit, the soup often seemed more water than substance, but the flavor was so appealing.

Delicious to the taste.

"I hear this place doesn't get enough business," a man told a woman at the next table. "They may have to close."

Brian sighed. So much misery. His favorite donut shop had gone out of business recently, too. And the independent movie theater where he sometimes went to see an R-rated movie without telling Lotte. It really was the Last Days. He left a twenty dollar tip on the table before he walked back to his car.

That meant no chocolates to stuff into Lotte's stocking. But then, chocolate had never been the aphrodisiac he'd been led to believe.

Was it a failure to give up on sex and just let Lotte be? Six months had passed since their last intercourse. Brian had tried giving his wife a back rub, massaging her neck and feet, drawing her a bubble bath. But each time, she looked so relaxed he felt it would be a betrayal to ask for anything in return.

He drove around Stanley Park for a while, a little icier than the rest of the city but still not bad, and then headed back home. Lotte was on the sofa, a fresh stack of novels on the coffee table in front of her, a smile on her lips. She waved perfunctorily as Brian walked into the room. Brian nodded and went back to his office to log onto Facebook again.

There was a post about Trudeau. One about politics in the U.S., another linking an article about a terrible forest fire in the Smoky Mountains that killed fourteen people. Investigators had just determined the fire to have been caused by arson.

And another test. "Oh, my God, you're killing me," he groaned out loud, instantly repentant over taking the Lord's name in vain. "I want to see how many of my friends read this to the end," the post began. "I want everyone to bear their testimony *and* tell one good thing they've done today to make the world a better place. Don't just Like or Share. Copy and paste into your own post if you have a real testimony of the gospel. #LighttheWorld."

So many tests. It was neverending. It wasn't enough that life itself offered so many, but his friends had to resort to testing one another all the time as well. It was the cyber equivalent to those old chain letters he used to get decades ago.

Brian highlighted the text and opened a new box for his own post. He pasted the words and started to write his testimony beneath them. "I know that The Church of Jesus Christ of Latter-day Saints is the true church," he typed. "I know that God lives. I know that the Book of Mormon is the word of God."

Then his fingers stopped, hovering over the keys. It would be just too gauche to tell about a good deed he'd done, especially since he'd done so few. Perhaps this was a test of his pride and ego. But how could it be? The Light the World campaign was Church-sponsored. Was *this* a test of faith?

Every day was test after test after test. His entire life was a chain letter, he realized. God had once been a man and forced to endure mortal life by *his* god, who'd had to do the same before him. Now Brian was here undergoing the test, and if he passed, he'd then force his own spirit children to face the same damn thing. Copying and pasting throughout eternity. The chain would never end.

Brian stared at the screen for a long moment, his heart racing for the first time in ages. His fingers twitched above the keyboard. Then he hit Delete. He turned off the computer and headed back out to the living room. He stood in front of the sofa until Lotte finally looked up at him. "Yes?" she asked, her finger holding her place in the book.

"How about I read to you for a while?" he asked.

Lotte frowned. She looked at the page in front of her, up at Brian, and back to the page. "All right," she said with a little shrug.

Brian sat on the sofa beside his wife. He took her feet in his lap and then the book from her hands. This was all he was going to get, he realized, and that would have to be okay. He still wanted to be with her.

But he wouldn't bother with the air freshener anymore. Lotte probably wouldn't notice one way or the other.

He cleared his throat and began to read.

Glory Hole Ethics

The young man poked Jesse in the chest with his index finger. "Fuck Trump!" he said, "And fuck you!" The man looked to be of mixed race, possibly part Latino and part black. One of the two young men with him was fully Latino, it appeared, and the other one white.

They all looked a little druggy, with stained clothing and unkempt hair and a couple of tattoos. The men glared at him angrily. Jesse was in White Center, perhaps the roughest part of Seattle, but he'd never had any problems before.

Jesse was confused over the verbal assault. Then he realized that because he was white, these guys thought he'd voted for Donald Trump. He thought about saying he'd voted for Clinton, but that wasn't true, either. He'd written in Evan McMullin's name on his King County ballot.

So maybe he *had* voted for Trump.

Jesse kept walking.

"Yeah, you *better* leave," the mixed-race man called after him.

Jesse continued on a couple of blocks until he reached the video store. Breanne didn't know he worked here yet, but the bishop knew. Bishop Menendez had asked him after Sacrament meeting a few weeks ago why his tithing had dropped so much.

"I quit my job at the bank," he explained.

"Why was that?"

"The loans they were asking me to make didn't feel ethical." We had quotas and needed to push people into borrowing money we knew they'd have trouble paying back.

"So where do you work now?"

"Fantasy Video."

That's when the bishop told him his temple recommend was being suspended.

"Hi, Jesse," said Sam when Jesse walked through the door. "I've counted out, so the drawer is yours."

Jesse was working his usual late shift today, from 4:30 to midnight. Working evenings was a pain in some ways, but it left his days open for job interviews if any came up. Not that he was trying very hard to find anything else. An adult video store might not be prestigious, but at least he didn't go home every day feeling dirty like he had at the bank. And it wasn't as if he had to hurry home to be with his family. Not anymore.

Breanne was telling everyone he kicked her out.

Jesse handed Sam a purple transfer slip for the bus. "Thanks, buddy," said Sam.

Jesse counted his till. $200. He waved goodbye as Sam hurried out the door. Then he counted the safe and made his first round checking the booths in the video arcade. He was just about to sit when a man came up to the counter and plopped a package of cock rings down.

"$14.95," said Jesse. "With tax, it comes to $16.39."

The customer gave him a twenty, collected his change, and walked out of the store. The door chimed as he went through. Two dead leaves blew into the building before the door shut.

Breanne had left Jesse two weeks after he quit the bank. "It's clear your wife and kids aren't a priority for you," she said. "I want a temple divorce so I can marry a man who puts his family first."

At least he'd been able to baptize Marcus. The boy had turned eight a month before Jesse left the bank. But neither Marcus nor his older sister Martina would speak to him anymore. Breanne had told them he didn't love them.

The house felt empty when he got home at 1:30, sometimes even a little later. That wouldn't last for long, though. Jesse and Breanne's first home was on the market so they could divide the asset equitably. When his wife left, she took their savings. Thankfully, Jesse had a separate account he'd never told her about. Did that make him a bad husband? Breanne also took their only car, but Jesse was already used to taking light rail, so he was okay about that.

But she'd taken their friends, too. Even the other elders in the Elders Quorum avoided him as if he were tainted by the pending divorce. He'd been friends with some of these men for eight years, ever since he and Breanne had moved into the ward.

Was it ethical for Jesse to provoke a divorce over finances, he wondered? Was it ethical for Breanne to demand a divorce over them? Well, maybe, thought Jesse. As a mother, her primary responsibility was to look out for the kids.

But shouldn't that have been his priority, too? Even more important than being able to look himself in the mirror?

A man eating a banana came into the store and started browsing through the gay DVDs with sticky hands. He knocked several cases onto the floor, picked them up, and then knocked several more off the shelf. He finally came up to the counter with two DVD cases.

"I'd like to buy these," he said. He aimed at the trash can behind the counter and threw the banana peel. It struck the side of the can and slid to the floor.

Jesse picked it up and placed it in the receptacle. Then he rang up the sale, retrieved two DVDs from a drawer, placed them in the cases, and ran the customer's credit card.

"Have an erotic day," Jesse said. It was the store's slogan. The boss had even hand printed a sign over the door which read, "Have an arotic day." Jesse didn't have the heart to tell him about the spelling.

A half hour passed. Jesse made another round through the arcade. While picking up a used tissue in one booth, he also found a $5 bill on the floor. He tossed the tissue and put the money in his pocket.

Should he try to get a job at another bank, he wondered? Would that bring Breanne and the kids back? Was it the right thing to do?

All Jesse ever wanted was to live a righteous life.

"Do you have any DVDs with she-males and women?" asked a black man about his own age, maybe thirty-five. "It's for my wife."

Sure, it is, thought Jesse. Of course, he didn't really care one way or the other. "Here's our trans section," he said, walking over and pointing to it. "You can browse, but I think most of these movies are she-males with men."

"Damn."

As a devout Mormon, Jesse had never watched any porn himself. Even after three months at the store, he still hadn't looked. But he felt that others should have the right if they wanted to exercise it. Neither did he feel any inclination to take advantage of the "ventilation openings" in the arcade booths, but he felt others had the right to sin if they chose. Wasn't that the whole purpose of the Plan of Salvation? To give people choices?

Breanne had the right to lie to their kids. He was just sorry he was going to lose them. He didn't particularly want to say anything mean back. Sometimes the rule, "If you can't say anything nice, don't say anything at all," was a good principle.

Jesse hadn't even said anything when he saw one of the men from the Elders Quorum go into the arcade one day. He thought at first he should tell the bishop but then decided against it. Was it ethical, though, not to tell the man's wife? For all he knew, of course, the wife already knew and gave her blessing.

Or was that just a cop-out?

A young man in his early twenties walked up to the counter. "I have some questions about anal," he said.

"Sure," said Jesse. "What do you want to know?"

"I've never done anything, but I want to try. Where do I start?"

By asking questions, thought Jesse. Most people were too afraid. But he was becoming a big fan of asking questions himself. He walked the customer over to the Anal section. "I'd get a butt plug first," he said. "Dildos are bigger. You can work up to that later."

"What about these things with ridges and bumps?" The young man pointed.

"That's to give your sphincter more stimulation. Almost all the pleasure from anal is from the sphincter."

Jesse had never tried anal himself, but his manager had given him a few pages with the FAQ customers asked. He knew what to say about the herbal supplements and the "cleaning solvents," too, including the importance of never using the word "poppers."

The young man picked out two butt plugs and placed them on the counter. Jesse rang them up and took the payment. "Did you want the black plastic bag or the clear one?" Jesse asked with a straight face.

"You're funny," the young man said. But he didn't look terribly amused. He took his bag and left.

Was it enough just to be pleasant, Jesse wondered? His next-door neighbor Janine had left two days ago for Standing Rock to join the protestors being gassed and shot with rubber bullets and hosed down in freezing weather. Now *that* was ethical.

Last week, Jesse had gone on the computer to give the cashier from Safeway a glowing review. When his bus driver had helped an obnoxious woman with her heavily loaded grocery cart get off the bus rather than just wait for her to manage it on her own, he'd written Metro to praise him.

Then he wondered if his note had helped the driver or instead hurt him. Maybe the man wasn't supposed to do things like that.

Jesse sold some magazines, a pump, and a vibrator. He checked the arcade. He sold a package of condoms. He checked the arcade again.

The job was easy enough. He'd even volunteered to work a double shift on Thanksgiving so the other employees could have the day off. The bishop was telling him he should marry again as soon as possible to avoid falling into any more sin, but since the divorce wasn't finalized, he was unable to attend Singles events officially. He had no desire to do so, anyway.

But despite still being married, he'd been invited by a rogue Single Adult rep to join the ward singles for a group holiday meal. "You need to start figuring out how to earn a woman's trust again," the rep for the ward told him. "Of course, if you come, we'll need to make an announcement to the ladies that you're not available just yet."

Jesse expected he'd feel better about life if he was at the store.

A heavyset man in shorts and a coat came in the store and started browsing through the "4 for $20" section. There were tiny red markings on the man's shorts.

"Are those crabs?" Jesse asked.

The man nodded.

"Better on the outside of your pants than the inside."

The man looked at Jesse and frowned.

Jesse understood why Jesus had spent so much time with thieves and prostitutes. There was a freedom here he never felt at church. Or at the bank, for that matter.

Was it ethical to feel happy while looking at a display of masturbators on the wall?

After 10:00, things started slowing down at the store. Jesse vacuumed the floor and wiped down all the glass cases. He rented a few movies to two different customers, made change for someone who needed one dollar bills for the arcade, and straightened the magazine racks. He made his last couple of rounds through the arcade and kicked out his last customer at 11:55. He counted his drawer and the safe, set the alarm, and left the building.

If White Center had been scary during the day, it felt even more ominous at night. Even at this hour, there was a bedraggled white woman begging for money at the intersection of Roxbury and 16th, holding a sign reading, "Army vet. Anything helps." A black man with a shaggy beard and torn leather jacket was smoking pot. An elderly Asian man was sleeping hunched over on a bus stop bench, a ripped plastic bag full of clothing at his feet.

The night was cold and windy, Jesse's favorite weather, so he didn't mind waiting twenty minutes for his first bus to Georgetown. He didn't mind waiting twenty-five minutes for the second one to Rainier Beach. But by the time he was waiting for his final bus up the hill, he began to feel weary.

How did one live an ethical life when one didn't have much of a life to begin with?

A Latina about twenty was also waiting for the bus, but she stood a good twenty-five feet away from Jesse, probably afraid of him, whether because he looked like a Trump supporter or just because he was a man, he didn't know.

Jesse heard some laughter and saw four young men crossing Rainier. He remembered the admonition against loud laughter. The men all looked to be in their mid-twenties. All of them were white, not a particularly common sight in this neighborhood at any time of the day. He wondered briefly if they'd driven down here from north Seattle. Was there a popular club nearby?

Jesse wouldn't know.

If he still obeyed the Word of Wisdom, still read his scriptures, was still active in the Church, and still paid his tithing, why couldn't he keep his temple recommend?

The four young men started making catcalls as they approached the Latina. She peered down the road for the bus.

"Hey, you! Go home!" shouted one of the men, laughing.

"Go back to Mexico!" said another. He pushed the girl on her shoulder. She started trying to walk toward Jesse, but the other two young men blocked her path.

"We have a new president now!" the first man said. "You're fucked!" He pushed the young woman, who bumped up against another young man, who pushed back.

"Please," said the woman.

"Hey, she speaks English!" said the first man, laughing. "Do you understand *this*?" He shoved her again. The woman stumbled.

Jesse walked calmly over to the group. It had to be done, whatever the consequences. The bus was still a good five minutes away. The woman might at least have a chance to run into the 24-hour grocery down the block. He reached forward and put his hand on the man's shoulder.

Leadership Roulette

It all began because Matt wanted to grow a beard. He'd just turned seventeen and started his senior year of high school, and he was talking with Bishop Rhodes in the bishop's office. It was time for Matt's biannual worthiness interview, his first with the new bishop.

"When was the last time you masturbated?" Bishop Rhodes asked.

Matt laughed. "This isn't my first time at the rodeo," he replied. "The question is, 'Are you keeping the Law of Chastity?'"

"That's what I asked."

"No, it isn't."

"Please answer the question, young man. If you don't, I'll already know the answer."

Matt laughed again. "I don't participate in self-abuse," he said with a grin. It was true enough. He didn't consider what he did with his penis abusive at all.

Bishop Rhodes harrumphed. "It's hard to believe a word you say when you're wearing that…that monstrosity." The bishop nodded toward him.

Matt was confused. He was wearing a white shirt and tie, just as he did every Sunday. "Excuse me?" he said.

"That disgusting beard," the bishop clarified. "You need to shave that filthy thing off today."

"I like my beard, Bishop. They even let me wear it at school if I keep it trim."

"School," the bishop said in disgust. "*This* is the house of the Lord."

"I thought the temple was the house of the Lord."

The bishop's eyes narrowed. "Young man, I'm sensing some hostility. As a judge in Zion, I have the power of discernment."

Discern this, Matt thought, sending a very specific message in the bishop's direction. "I'll shave it off when I go on a mission next year," he said, "but I want to keep it for now."

He was about to say it would discourage young women in the ward from going out with him, which would help keep him pure for his mission, but before he had a chance, Bishop Rhodes slapped his desk, sending his Salt Lake temple paperweight jumping. "In that case," the man said, "you leave me no choice. You are no longer to bless the sacrament, and I'm banning you from next Saturday's youth temple trip. You will not be going to Mesa."

Matt's mouth fell open.

"Let me know when you're ready to repent." The bishop dismissed the boy with a wave of his hand.

Matt walked out of the office and down the hall toward the foyer. Bishop Welker had been a great guy, he thought. Too bad he'd been released two months ago. Matt had frequently heard his parents talk about "Leadership Roulette," the unpredictability of temperament in successive bishops or stake presidents.

He joined his folks in the lobby, and together they went out to the car. They'd waited patiently for him, even though he was the fourth interview after three long hours of meetings.

In the car on the way home, Matt told his parents what had happened, focusing on the part about the rewritten morality question. His father had explained to him during "the talk" a few years earlier that there was nothing wrong with masturbation, and Matt could often hear his parents in their bedroom down the hall when they had sex, though most of the noise seemed to come from his father. In any event, the topic wasn't taboo in their house. But that wasn't the part of the interview which seemed to set off Matt's father.

"That imbecile," he said. "Doesn't he know Jesus wore a beard? And Brigham Young? And—"

"Now, dear," said Matt's mother. "We're not to speak ill of the Lord's anointed."

"Do you think Bishop Rhodes is right, Mom?" Matt asked from the back seat.

"Well…" His mother opened her purse and looked inside it for several moments.

"Yes?" prompted his father.

"Sister Williams told me what he said to her a few weeks ago," she said carefully, "and it seemed a little harsh."

Matt knew Sister Williams' nine-year-old daughter had died of leukemia the week after Bishop Rhodes was called.

"He told Barbara he wouldn't renew her temple recommend until she caught up with her tithing. She explained about the medical bills, but he was adamant. He told her that unless she stopped procrastinating and paid her tithing right then, she'd never see her daughter again."

"That's awful, Mom."

She shrugged. "Maybe Bishop Rhodes receives specific inspiration for the members of the ward. We really can't question."

"I'm not shaving my beard," Matt said.

There was silence in the car for a moment. Then Matt's father spoke up. "The trick's on him," he said. "The bishop will be out of town next weekend. You can go on the temple trip, and no one will be the wiser."

"Devin!" said Matt's mother.

"Amy!" said Matt's father.

"Good," said Matt. "I love doing baptisms for the dead. Makes me feel like I'm making a difference in the world."

But things didn't go as smoothly the next Saturday as Matt had hoped. Bishop Rhodes did show up at the meetinghouse as the youth were gathering. When he saw

Matt climbing into a van with some other teenagers, he ran up to the vehicle and slapped the side.

"What do you think you're doing, young man?" he bellowed. "I specifically told you you were not to go to the temple until you shaved off that beard. I will *not* have you defy me!"

"I'll just sit in the temple foyer," Matt said, trying to think on his feet. "Or maybe sit out by the reflecting pool. At least I'll still get to feel the Spirit."

"You won't feel the Spirit no matter where you are," the bishop replied, "until you repent of your rebellious attitude. You're like Laman and Lemuel. You're like Korihor. You're like…like…"

"Alma the Younger?" prompted Matt.

"Get out of that van and go home this minute!"

Matt climbed back out of the van and called his mother to come pick him up.

The next day at church, since Bishop Rhodes had finally left town for a few days, Matt went to sit behind the sacrament table. He'd been sitting there less than two minutes when Brother Caldwell, the first counselor in the bishopric, walked over.

"You can't sit there as long as you have that beard," he said. "Bishop Rhodes left me strict instructions." The man spoke loudly. Matt could tell the families sitting in the first few pews could hear him.

He smiled pleasantly and stood up. But while Sister McKenzie was offering the opening prayer a few minutes later, Matt walked quietly back up onto the platform.

He opened the door to the tiny room where the sacrament trays were stored and closed it softly behind him. Then when he heard the sacrament hymn being sung a few minutes later, he came out and stood off to the side near Stephen and Craig, his two friends blessing the bread and water that day.

Matt stood motionless as first one priest and then the other read the prayer cards. Looking out over the congregation, he could see several frowning faces. He didn't bother to look in Brother Caldwell's direction. As soon as the deacons returned the trays, Matt walked down and sat next to his parents about ten rows back.

His father winked at him, but his mother had her hand over her face, her head bowed. Matt imagined he could hear several people in the congregation murmuring about him, but then he realized they were probably just trying to quiet their eternally squirming kids.

The following Sunday, Bishop Rhodes was in the foyer waiting for Matt. "Brother and Sister Slater, you two go on into the chapel," he told Matt's parents. "I need to have a little chat with your son."

"Did you have a nice trip last weekend?" Matt asked.

The bishop's eyes narrowed. "You are not allowed in the chapel today," he said. "You are not to partake of the sacrament. I will *not* have you defying me."

"Okay," Matt said agreeably. "I'll just sit on the sofa until it's time for Sunday School." He smiled at the bishop and walked nonchalantly to the other side of the foyer. As soon as Bishop Rhodes walked into the chapel, he pulled out his phone and sent a text.

His friend Stephen was blessing the sacrament again this week, and Stephen's younger brother Danny was one of the deacons passing it. At Stephen's direction, Danny added the foyer to his designated route, and Matt took a piece of bread and a tiny cup of water. He didn't tell his parents what the bishop had said.

The following Sunday, Bishop Rhodes again stopped Matt from entering the chapel. This time, he wouldn't let Stephen or Danny in, either. After the bishop stalked through the doors, Matt returned to his dad's car and pulled a corkboard out of the trunk. He set it up in the foyer, with photos of Brigham Young, John Taylor, Wilford Woodruff, Lorenzo Snow, Joseph F. Smith, Heber J. Grant, and George Albert Smith pinned to it.

The photocopies were all black and white, but Matt had colored the beards of each prophet: red for Brigham Young, orange for John Taylor, yellow for Wilford Woodruff, and so on down the line. Several young children pointed, but their parents quickly herded them into the chapel.

Matt saw Brother Maddow with stubble on his face walk by with a smirk, and he took a slow, deep breath to calm down. Such a double standard. Grown men could always get away with things kids couldn't do.

After services, Bishop Rhodes walked up to Matt. "In my office," he said. "Now."

"Sure thing, Bishop. Just let me put this back in the car first." Matt walked out of the building and waited by the family car until the next two hours of meetings were over.

The Sunday after that, Bishop Rhodes did not try to prevent Matt from entering the chapel. Because Stephen and Craig were blessing the sacrament again, Matt sat with his parents, about eight rows back. After the opening hymn, the bishop stood and spoke firmly into the microphone.

"We're going to sing the opening hymn again," he said. "You did not sing it with enough zeal. There are far too many members of this congregation who are taking a lackadaisical approach to the gospel. Sister Warren, please play the hymn another time."

The congregation sang the song once more, and then Brother Delridge offered an opening prayer. After that, the bishop stood up again.

"It has come to my attention that there is a wicked, rebellious attitude among our youth here," he began, "and the main instigator seems to be Matt Slater." He pointed directly at Matt, who looked up from his phone. "Look at that sloppy, ugly beard. I would like each of you to talk to this boy. I can't seem to get through to him. But perhaps all of us working together may yet save his soul."

He sat down, and there was a stunned silence in the room. Even the young children who were usually fussy were still.

Then Brother Maddow stood up, a row ahead of Matt. The man's stubble had grown into a short beard over the past week. Matt stared at him in confusion. Then Brother McKenzie stood, and Matt realized he had a fresh, trim beard as well. Brother Matthews stood, and Brother Cooper, both with brand new, trim beards.

Matt had been so focused on himself lately he hadn't noticed what some of the congregants were doing for him. Before long, fifteen men stood in various pews throughout the chapel, all with newly grown beards. No one said a word.

Except for Bishop Rhodes. But most of what he said wasn't fit for the ears of some of the younger congregants. Brother Caldwell had to lead him out of the chapel with the help of Brother Hodderson, the second counselor.

As soon as the chapel doors were closed behind the bishopric, the men all sat back in their pews. Brother Ayers, the ward clerk, stood up and directed the remainder of the service. It was Fast and Testimony meeting, and Matt vowed in front of everyone to be the best missionary he could be when he left at the end of the school year. Several bearded men were among those nodding their approval.

Matt hoped he got a good mission president. It had never occurred to him before that he might not.

But he vowed to himself he'd never complain even once about the mandatory missionary haircut, no matter what the man was like.

He hoped he could keep his promise.

Maybe he'd bring an electric razor just in case, so he could shave his head if he needed to make a statement.

Perhaps it didn't even matter what number his ball landed on the next time he played leadership roulette. He could bet on both black and red.

And maybe green, too.

Matt smiled and sat back down with his family, which was much larger now than he'd ever realized before.

Working Out

Things were finally beginning to work out for Miranda. She smiled and peered through the blinds to the Time Saver across the street. She'd been fired from her job as a receptionist for an eye surgeon shortly after she'd moved into the apartment upstairs, undoubtedly because one of those mean girls at the nursing school had called to tell them she'd been kicked out.

But then miraculously, the manager of the apartment complex told her she was quitting and asked if Miranda wanted the job. She passed the interview without hardly even flirting, moved into the apartment/office downstairs, was given free rent and utilities, plus was paid $800 a month. She'd been the manager for two months now without a problem, and maybe life was going to turn out all right, after all. She wasn't quite sure if it meant God was finally blessing her or if it was just luck.

There was a knock at the door, and Miranda opened it. A young woman about twenty-three stood in the hall. She was blond and probably a size two. Miranda could tell instantly she was trash. She could always tell about other women. She had an easy guide. If she thought it was someone Keith would probably pick up on Bourbon Street, then the woman was trash.

"Can I help you?"

"I was wondering if you had any vacancies? For a one-bedroom?"

The last thing Miranda wanted was for a slut like this to live in the complex, but she got points for filling up apartments, so she couldn't turn her down. It seemed a bit flashy to want a one-bedroom instead of an efficiency, though. The girl probably had a sugar daddy. At least that meant she wouldn't come on to Keith if they met in the hallway while Keith was over making one of his visits.

"Sure," Miranda said sweetly. "Come on in and fill out an application."

After the sleazy tramp left, Miranda put the application aside to give to the building owner later, and she got back to her work. She finished her typing and filing for the day and then pulled out her Thighmaster and exercised for a few minutes. She also had some five-pound weights she regularly lifted while on the phone, and some ten-pound weights she lifted maybe twice a week when she really felt in the mood to work out her frustrations.

She wouldn't need that if Keith would just step up to the plate and marry her. She fasted twice a month for that, for how many years now? What would it take to convince God to bless her? She knew she just had to show God she was willing to endure to the end, and now that Keith was finishing school, she'd done that.

Miranda's weight kept going up and down as she skipped meals and dieted and then ate fatty foods, but she was still a size fourteen, almost a sixteen, and at the age of thirty-two, there wasn't much chance of getting married if Keith didn't ask her. But he would.

He was almost finished anesthesiology school and would be leaving New Orleans and moving to Alexandria for a new job after he graduated next week. He kept insisting he wasn't going to take her with him, but Miranda knew he would. And obviously the only way he could get her to go was by marrying her. Things were looking up. Soon she could kiss this dead-end job goodbye.

Miranda squeezed some handsprings for a couple of minutes, but the handles were hard plastic and hurt her fingers, so she put them down and looked out the window again. Keith had only come over here once during the daytime since she moved in, usually preferring the dark when no one would see him, but she kept hoping.

Of course, that one time during the day hadn't been a very pleasant experience. She was on the phone last week with the exterminator for the complex, and Keith had barged in, furious from a letter Miranda had just mailed him. He picked up pencils and pads from her desk and threw them at her as she talked on the phone, whispering, "I'll have your job! You wait and see! I'll get you fired for harassing me!"

But *he* was always the one who called, usually after 11:00, saying he'd be over soon to sleep with her. Though that wasn't the term he used. And like always, he ripped her clothes off as soon as he came in the door. She still couldn't bear to let him come in her mouth, and she refused to let him do anal sex to her, so almost every time they had sex, he criticized her the whole time.

But he kept coming, didn't he? So Miranda knew he really loved her. Why else would he keep seeing her for sex after seven years, if he truly hated the sex?

He might actually try to get her fired, though, just so he could pretend he had to take her in because Miranda had nowhere to go. He wouldn't want people to think he loved her, after telling everyone for years he didn't, but he'd marry her, and she'd know the truth.

Once, he'd even let slip that he might take her as a wife, though he quickly joked that he'd keep her locked up in the attic, but it was too late. He'd let it out, and she knew how he really felt. And how could she ignore the fact that seven years was how long Jacob had worked to marry Leah, and that he'd worked seven more years for Rachel? Miranda had now worked seven years for Keith, and God simply had to hand him over. It was only fair.

There was another knock on the door. When Miranda opened it, she saw the creepy thirty-five-year-old man who lived in B-214. A few days ago she'd left her laundry in the dryer and went back to her apartment to wait for it to finish, and when she'd gone back, she found two of her panties missing. And the guy from B-214 had been walking across the parking lot then, pretending he didn't see her.

She'd used her key to get in his apartment the next day when he was at work, but she didn't find anything. Still, she knew it was him. He probably sold the panties to a friend, or brought them to work to fondle during his lunch break or something.

"Can I help you?"

"I'm Bruce from B-214."

"Yes, I know."

"My kitchen faucet is leaking. And my garbage disposal doesn't work."

"Okay. I'll report it to maintenance."

"Thanks."

"No problem."

The man hesitated a moment, so Miranda didn't close the door. "You know," he said shyly, "you're the nicest manager we've had in a long time. I hope you stay a while."

"Thank you," Miranda said curtly, closing the door in his face.

So that's what happened to the panties. After that pervert had sniffed them or done some other ungodly thing with them, he'd put them down the garbage disposal. Why else would it be broken? Garbage disposals didn't just break. What a creep. And with the admission that he liked her, it was clear now he was stalking her. Men were just dogs.

But Miranda dutifully noted the complaints and called the maintenance guy to let him know about them. Of course, the maintenance man had leered at her a couple of times, too, so she didn't like him, either.

Miranda was about to turn and go back to her desk when she looked through the window and saw two men in white shirts and ties step out of a car in front of the Time Saver. She gasped and stepped back from the blinds but kept looking.

That was Elder Andrews! What was he doing here? She'd had a mild fling with the twenty-year-old Mormon missionary a few months earlier while she was staying with her friend Bonnie right after being kicked out of nursing school.

Bonnie had sex or at least petted with Elder Peterson, Andrews's companion, almost every night when the two missionaries came over at 10:30 to watch movie videos. They rented a room in the garage behind Bonnie's house. After a while, Elder Andrews had made his move on Miranda, and they kissed while the movie played.

But then Miranda found out he was really after Bonnie, and then Bonnie's mother had told him lies about Miranda, and it was all a big mess. Now Bonnie had moved to Utah to try her luck with Peterson, who had finished his mission, and so what was Andrews doing here? He knew she lived here; he'd helped her move. Was he checking up on her?

Then Miranda remembered the two elders she'd seen at the Time Saver a month ago. It was 10:30 at night when she first noticed them, and the rules said they were supposed to be in bed by then. But they went inside the convenience store and played pinball until 11:00, looking out through the window at Miranda's apartment the whole time.

Around 11:30, they came outside and looked directly across the street. Then they'd looked disgusted, made a phone call, and left.

Had they been spying on her? Were they checking for the bishop to see if Keith came over? Had Keith been the one to get them to spy on her? Was he really married, and it was his wife was checking up on him? Had Bonnie's mother said something? Was it someone from the nursing school? It could be anyone, but it was almost certainly the Church.

Years earlier when she'd been attending her ward, back when Keith was separating from his wife, Miranda had seen Karen leave the chapel with her baby once, leaving her purse on the pew. Of course, even then, while Keith was having an affair with Miranda, he'd started nasty rumors about Karen that everyone believed, and Miranda had seen with her own eyes as the bishop's wife, who babysat for Karen's little girl, leaned over and looked through Karen's purse while she was gone.

And while Miranda was staying with the Robertsons, Brother Robertson would say he had to go out on an assignment from the bishop and spy on some church member. So Miranda knew it went on.

Miranda had eventually forgotten about the two elders from a month ago, but what could she possibly think now? The elders went inside and played pinball, but they kept looking across the street. And she knew these two were aware she lived here, whether the others last time had known or not.

Miranda sat on the sofa with her hand on her chest. What was she going to do?

She went to her desk and picked up the phone. Keith had forbidden her to call during the day or after 11:00 at night, but now that his classes were over, it wouldn't matter, so she dialed his number. The answering machine clicked on.

"If you're a friend, leave a message. If you're not, I've got this place booby trapped. If you know me, you know it's true. Beep."

Miranda rolled her eyes. Every time she heard one of his stupid Rambo messages, she remembered the times they'd had sex at his place and she found either a knife or a gun under his pillow. He'd joked that they were there in case he ever finally got tired of her. She knew the purpose of life was to start on the pathway to perfection, and she marveled sometimes at how far Keith still had to go. He threw this same point in *her* face all the time, too.

"We're supposed to be working toward perfection," he'd say. "If we're going to have eternal sex, you sure have a long way to go before you're perfect at it." But she wasn't concerned about any of that now. She had something important to tell him. "Keith, your spies are across the street. Give me a call."

She felt better then, glanced out the window again, and went back to her desk and found something to do. She liked to stay ahead of schedule in case her boss came to the complex to check up on her. The maid had been fired a couple of weeks back for leaving the vacuum cleaner in the hallway overnight, where it was stolen.

Well, that was the *official* reason they gave, but Miranda knew that the maid had reported seeing the maintenance man with his pants down when she'd gone in to an unoccupied apartment. His back was to her, and when he heard the door, he zipped right up. The maid didn't know if he was just stuffing his shirt in or what, but she'd told Miranda, and Miranda had told her boss.

The maintenance man was still here, and the maid was fired. That's the way it always was. Men simply got away with everything, and women paid the price. Miranda wanted to make sure she was doing her job well so they couldn't do that to her.

Keith didn't call back, but he showed up at 11:30, knocking abruptly on the door. Miranda was half asleep, and the first thing that came to her mind was that another drunk from the bar next to the Time Saver had come into the building. The first week after she'd become manager, some guy had pushed his hand through a window trying to get in, and then he'd bled all over the stairwell and the sidewalk. Men were such creeps. But after a moment, Miranda realized someone was calling her name.

Her eyes opened wide and she leaped off of the sofa and hurried to the door. Keith hated to be kept waiting. He didn't like anyone seeing him in the hall. She undid the chain and let him in.

Keith shut the door, locked it, and then stood staring at Miranda in her pajamas, with an odd look in his eyes. "What the hell is going on?" he demanded.

"There were two missionaries across the street. They stayed out there for two hours. I was just wondering if you sent them to check up on me."

Keith put his hand on his forehead and shook his head slowly. "And what would I be expecting to find while you're at work?"

"I don't know. They were out there till 11:30 one night. They might even be out there right now." Feeling a sudden thrill, she rushed to the window and looked out, but the elders were gone. She knew that Keith denied to everyone he was seeing her. She wished someone else could find him here to back her up.

"Well, since I'm here, take off those clothes," Keith ordered.

"No," said Miranda, sitting on the sofa. "Let's talk first. We never talk. I want to tell you what I read in the Book of Mormon this week." That should cool him down for a couple of minutes.

Keith sighed. "Take off the clothes or I'm leaving."

Miranda looked down at the floor. She knew he would, but she also knew she only had a week left to work out a way to get him to propose. "You just need to get me in the mood is all. You know it takes women a little longer." Why was he always so mean? Why was he pretending he didn't he understand?

He walked over to the sofa, and standing before her, he unzipped and pulled out his erect penis. She felt like dirt and wanted to hit him. Then he put his hands on the back of her head and pulled her forward. "This will get you in the mood." She resisted, but he pulled her forward again.

He was gone twenty minutes later, and Miranda put her clothes back on. She lay on the sofa and looked at the slivers of the Time Saver sign she could see through the blinds. One more week, she thought, before he graduated and left New Orleans, and yet Keith sometimes waited two weeks between visits. She'd have to come up with some special way to get him back over. Thinking of various plans she might try, she slowly fell asleep.

Miranda woke up with a smile, knowing now how to get Keith to come back over. She'd tell him she joined a health club. He'd see she was seriously trying to lose weight, and he'd come to see her again. He was horny all the time. It wouldn't take much.

She had, in fact, been thinking a great deal about joining a gym. After all, there was one just a couple of blocks away, the big one that the Metairie bishop owned. The fact that a Mormon owned it was what kept her from joining sooner, but now that was something in its favor. She wanted the Church to see that she was a strong, independent woman who didn't need them or a man to make her happy.

And if Keith ever came by the gym to see if she was really working out, they'd see that he *was* interested in her, despite what he told everybody. Maybe the bishop himself would even be there to see Keith. It would be wonderful.

At 5:00, as soon as Miranda got off work, she walked down the street to join. It cost a good bit, she realized with a bit of surprise, irritated that the bishop was probably a millionaire. The Church always seemed to get successful businessmen to be their leaders. That was why there was no spirit in church. It was run like a business. A business that always favored men.

And she hated herself for giving her own hard-earned money to a rich Mormon when she still had $200 in NSF checks to pay back to the bank from when she lost her last job. But this was an investment that would pay off quickly, so she went in and worked out for half an hour.

Miranda was still wearing her make-up since she'd just gotten off work, but no one at a health club would be interested in such an obviously out-of-shape woman, so she didn't even look twice at the men. There was that grotesquely fat man over there, but even if he was interested, Miranda certainly wasn't. And that other guy wasn't too out of shape, but God, he was ugly.

Then a cute guy glanced in her direction and smiled, but Miranda immediately looked away, not wanting to see the disgust and rejection in his face when he finally got a good look at her. Besides, she realized, he wasn't really all that attractive, after all.

There were few men really who were as good looking as Keith. His hair was starting to thin a little these days, and she hated bald men, but she'd put so much into this relationship already that she didn't feel she could give up now.

She'd gone out on one blind date while she was living in the nursing dorm, hoping to make Keith jealous, but the guy had turned out to be a real dork, and at the end of the evening, he admitted he had a girlfriend waiting for him at home. Most of the male nursing students were gay, so they were out of the question, and who did that leave? Miranda didn't really know how to meet other guys, and what other way was there to make Keith propose?

She wasn't about to go to a bar, she'd die before she went to a Singles meeting at church, only losers used personals ads or went to Matchmaker, and she wasn't allowed to date anyone in her building, so what other options did she have?

She tried to do her grocery shopping right after work while she was still dressed nicely, hearing she could meet some guys there, but only one guy had ever looked interested, a slimy looking Italian guy with gold chains and his shirt half unbuttoned, who squeezed some melons while smirking creepily at her.

He made Keith seem like a gentleman. She wondered sometimes why she put up with Keith, but he really was about the best thing out there, and she knew she'd never really love anyone else.

Keith never used condoms, but Miranda still never managed to get pregnant, though she'd told him several times, of course, that she was. She wondered if something was wrong with her and she'd never get pregnant, or if God was just waiting for the right moment.

She'd felt sure if she became a nurse like Keith was that he'd want her, but when she'd called in tears after failing her pharmacology test and being kicked out, he'd just said coldly, "I knew you were too stupid to make it."

He'd *promised* to help her study when she enrolled, but he never did, not even once. And now he was going to be making even more money as an anesthetist, and he said that even a nurse didn't make enough for him to marry anymore.

He'd probably still screw around even if they were married, of course. He'd screwed around on Karen, and he said he was having sex with other women anesthetists and women doctors now. But as long as Miranda got to be #1 by being his wife, everything else would be okay. It would definitely be better than living alone. Besides, once they were married, she'd find ways of keeping him home. She wasn't stupid.

After exercising for half an hour, Miranda walked past the rows of other people working out and strolled back to her apartment. As she reached the Time Saver, she decided to go in and buy a Coke, but as she walked in the door, she realized the two elders were in back playing pinball.

She surely looked frumpy after the exercising, but at least she still had on some make-up. She walked up and down the aisles, pretending to be looking for something, trying to get close enough so that Elder Andrews could say something to her, since she wasn't about to make the first move.

But as she walked nearer, out of the corner of her eye, she saw the two duck down and hide. So they *were* spying! They weren't here just because they had an apartment down the street, like she had considered. They probably lived miles away. They were clearly here for her! She stopped in her tracks, wondering what to do now. Then she heard them giggling. That seemed rather odd.

"She must be crazy!" she heard Elder Andrews whisper. "After what she said about me!" And the two young men giggled again.

Miranda tried not to look as if she heard them and instead quickly walked up to the counter with her Coke and left. How could he *say* that? She wanted to run back to her apartment as fast as she could but made herself walk slowly so they wouldn't think anything was wrong.

She kept hearing Andrews over and over in her head, and as soon as she closed the door behind her, she threw the Coke in the sink, where the can split and brown liquid fizzled everywhere, and she opened her mouth in a cry that never came out.

Why had he said such a thing? What could it possibly mean? She'd never said anything at all about him. Bonnie's mother must have told him more lies before he was transferred over here.

Why did people do this to her all the time? What had she ever done to them? They treated her like she was a freak. What in the world was wrong with everybody?

She looked at the Coke spilled everywhere and closed her eyes. She'd have to call Keith and tell him what Elder Andrews had said.

Suddenly, she opened her eyes again and smiled. Why, yes, that would work out just right, she thought, smiling even more broadly. She'd call Keith to tell him about the missionaries, and she'd only mention in passing that she was on her way home from the gym. That way, he'd hear about the gym without thinking she was trying to impress him!

That was perfect, she realized, even better than she'd hoped. He'd feel sorry for her, come over to comfort her, plus see that she was trying to get in better shape. Only six more days, but she'd get him. And she'd make up something about a businessman in a suit in line at the checkout counter flirting with her, perhaps dangerously so, just to make sure she caught Keith's attention.

Miranda almost skipped to her phone and danced a little as she dialed. Listening to Keith's recorded message, she wiped her smile off and tried to get in the right mood again. She tried to sound frantic, almost suicidal, as she told the machine what had happened. Then she hung up and sighed happily. She hummed a little tune as she walked back to her kitchen to clean up the mess.

She tried to do a little extra cleaning around the apartment, too. Then she took a shower and put her make-up on again, even though applying it took ninety minutes, so she'd be ready when Keith showed up in the middle of the night. She even skipped dinner tonight to lose a few extra ounces.

Keith would see. With the proper incentive, she could be a great person. She'd be absolutely wonderful if only he would just marry her. And he *would* marry her, soon.

Yes, she thought happily, straightening up the Church books on her bedside stand. Things were finally working out. Men were pigs, and God was a man, but even God would have to come around and bless her eventually. She had six days to enact her plan. God had made the world in six days. Miranda could make a husband.

Keith thought she was stupid, but she'd show him she was smart enough to get what she wanted. He'd never even know what hit him. She rehearsed in her mind how to casually describe the businessman at the Time Saver so it would sound like she wasn't even really thinking about that part of her encounter in the store.

She wished there were someone she could call to confide in about what she was doing, maybe rehearse with them a little. But she didn't know anyone. So she prayed instead.

"God, I realize you're a man, but you're a *perfect* man, so I know you understand."

And she smiled, sitting on the edge of her bed, waiting for the wonderful night to come.

Zombies for Jesus

"Do what you're told," Cliff said to his fifteen-year-old son, Jon, who was pulling the covers over his head. Cliff leaned over and ripped them back off.

"But Dad," Jon protested, sitting up, "I hate Seminary. Everyone walks around in a daze all the time half-asleep. I gave it a year as I promised. I don't want to do it anymore."

"We all do things we don't want to do. You think I want to go to work every day?"

Jon rolled his eyes. "But Dad, you *have* to do that. I don't have to go to Seminary."

"You do if you want your allowance."

"Jeez, sometimes you make me wish I was dead."

"You will be soon enough. Life is short. It's eternity we have to worry about."

Jon rolled his eyes again.

Cliff walked out to the kitchen, irritated. Did Jon think he liked teaching early morning Seminary himself? Cliff didn't have to be at work at the university until 9:00, and the Church was making him get up at 5:30 every morning so he could teach the teenagers at 6:00. Cliff hated teaching, which was why he'd gone into Information Technology in college in the first place. He hated teenagers, too.

Sometimes, that even included Jon, his oldest. And ever since his time as a missionary, he hated waking up early. The kids weren't the only ones walking around in a daze.

But the bishop had called Cliff to this position five years ago, so what could he do? A call from the bishop was a call from God. Cliff couldn't let Jesus down.

Of course, today Cliff had more important things on his mind than the early Church history he was teaching. It was all fine and good that tens of thousands of people had followed Brigham Young across the plains without a second thought. Cliff was facing a layoff at work today, and getting laid off would definitely require a second thought from him. Maybe even a third as well.

Cliff had followed Mormon teachings faithfully his whole life, of course. Surely, God wouldn't abandon him now. Although there were a hundred layoffs to be announced at the university today, there would be only one layoff in Cliff's department, and God wouldn't let it be him.

"Hurry it up, Jon," Cliff called out as he drank his orange juice.

"Good grief, Cliff," Elizabeth said, walking into the kitchen, still groggy. "You're going to wake the dead. The rest of us don't have to get up at this ungodly hour, you know."

"Sorry." Cliff wasn't too sympathetic toward Liz and their other children sleeping in. After Liz got the kids off to school, Cliff knew she always went back to sleep for another hour. She'd resisted the Church pushing her to be a stay-at-home mom when they first married, but after a few years of it, Liz had resigned herself to a rote existence. Cliff resented that she still found ways to take it out on him, though. He'd have loved to have such a carefree life of his own, napping whenever he wanted.

In class this morning, Cliff told the students about the wagon train that had set out across the plains too late in the season, against the prophet's directives, and become bogged down in the snow. "Thus we see how important it is to follow the instructions of our leaders," Cliff explained.

A hand shot up. "Brother Carlyle," said Andy, a friend of Jon's. "Didn't God want the Saints to get out to Salt Lake quickly? I mean, if they have to wait an extra five months in Illinois before going, who benefits from that? Couldn't God just have kept the snow back another couple of weeks?"

"There are natural laws we have to live with," Cliff said.

"Are you telling me God can't control the weather? I thought He split the Red Sea. I thought He brought the seagulls to Salt Lake to eat the crickets. I thought He brought earthquakes upon the Nephites. Can't God do anything He wants?"

"The prophet had spoken," Cliff said. "That was God's way of saying to do it that way."

"You mean God let those pioneers die just so the prophet could save face and be right?"

Cliff sighed. Teenagers, he grumbled to himself. They thought they knew everything. "We don't question God's actions."

"Then how do we understand Him?"

"We don't delve into the mysteries. The prophet tells us to stick to the plain and simple truths of the gospel."

"So we have to be mindless sheep?" Andy asked. "I thought the Church's motto was 'the glory of God is intelligence.'"

"I'm tired of this discussion," said Cliff. "Let's get back to the lesson."

He did return to the manual, but Andy's words irritated him, sticking into his mind like a splinter in the skin of his finger. There'd been a time when Cliff believed that intelligence was a good thing. He'd worked hard in school, naturally, but it was more than that.

He used to read books about Lincoln and the Arctic and Henry the Fifth. He used to watch documentaries about the Louvre and continental drift and Native American Indians. He used to lie outside and look at the stars.

Packing up his teaching materials at the end of the lesson, Cliff wondered how long it had been since he'd read a book. With a full-time job and four kids, who had time?

Then again, when was the last time he'd even thought about it? Cliff knew that as a god one day, he would have to learn *everything*. He used to want to start the process now. There used to be a time when he felt a person couldn't even inherit the Celestial Kingdom in the first place and have the privilege to finally learn all things unless he made an effort here to take advantage of every opportunity for learning that this life provided. What had happened?

Cliff drove Jon to school, not wanting to talk to him on the drive, still mad at his friend, Andy. Cliff remembered how after Liz had suffered so much during her pregnancy with Jon, she'd never wanted to bear any more children. Cliff had badgered her, repeating again and again how it was God's will, it was a commandment, it was an essential part of God's plan, it was what Mormons did. She'd relented unhappily, but it had resulted in far less sex for Cliff over the years.

We all do things we don't want to do, Cliff thought. Doing what you were told without asking why was the real ticket to heaven.

"See you, Dad."

Cliff grunted as Jon stepped out of the car.

"Have a good day at work."

"Yep."

Cliff drove off, arriving at the university an hour early, as usual. He logged onto the computer, but instead of playing a game, he checked the news. He hardly ever watched the news anymore. There was fighting in the Congo, he saw now, a murder-suicide in Texas, and a volcano in the Philippines.

Boring.

Cliff was about to click back to his game, Zombie Killers, when he stopped himself.

Why was all that drama boring to him, he suddenly wondered. Then he wondered at the fact that he'd been able to wonder again. It had been a long time.

The flicker of life in his brain intrigued him. It reminded him of the time years ago when he used to dream of creating new inventions. Over the years, as he watched others come up with the MP3 and iPod and Wii and everything else, Cliff felt that life was passing him by. But he couldn't make himself sit down and study enough to do anything creative.

Even just keeping up with the constant changes in computer technology was almost more than he could bear. Cliff wished he could simply relax and coast for a while. He was so tired all the time. He refused to take antihistamines because they made him feel foggy, but he had to admit, he felt foggy most of the time, anyway.

"Morning, Cliff," said his supervisor, Sandria, coming into the office.

"Good morning."

"Still getting here early?" she asked wryly. "Trying to ward off the evil eye of layoffs?"

"You know me. Can't wait to get to work every day."

Sandria laughed. "Well, there's a call here from Professor Ryan. Got locked out of Blackboard again. Can you go over and train him yet another time?"

"Sure thing."

Cliff hated dealing with Professor Ryan. He was first counselor in the stake presidency, and though Cliff was going out of his way to be patient with the man's Luddite tendencies, Ryan always seemed to be judging Cliff, continually making Cliff feel he was being reported on back to the stake president.

Was he the reason why Cliff never got any real substantial calling at church? Was Cliff not conforming enough? Were all Ryan's supposed computer problems just chances at getting Cliff close enough to spy on?

"Hi, Brother Carlyle," Dr. Ryan said as Cliff entered the professor's office. "How's that early morning Seminary coming along?"

"Fine."

"Good, good." He paused, and there was an awkward silence. "Hey, got your garden planted yet?"

Cliff nodded curtly. He hated gardening, but it was a commandment to grow as many of your own vegetables as you could. He hated lots of things that seemed uniquely Mormon commandments. Cliff had dutifully researched his genealogy despite finding it utterly boring.

He wrote in his journal regularly, though since he wasn't at all literary, the entries were less and less interesting as time went by. Some days, he just wrote about his latest Zombie Killer adventure. But he wrote, as he was told to do.

"Let's get you back up on Blackboard," Cliff said, trying to focus on business.

Before long, Dr. Ryan assured Cliff that he "got it this time," and promised to write him a good recommendation if he was laid off later in the day.

"You couldn't pray so that I won't get laid off to begin with?" asked Cliff. "What good is it to be close to God if you don't have any say?"

Dr. Ryan laughed but broke off when he saw Cliff wasn't laughing with him. "God can't *make* people be good and do the right thing," he said.

Cliff frowned. Why not, he thought. The Church forced *him* to do what it wanted all the time. He wore his white shirt to church every week, held Family Home Evening every Monday that his kids dreaded, home taught the families that put up with his visits for the same reason he made them, to check another item off the list of requirements for being a dedicated Mormon.

Cliff had been so excited to be sent to Alaska on his mission twenty years earlier. It would be exotic, he thought. He could see the way other people did things. But the Church had been exactly the same in Alaska as it was back home. People wore the same clothes to church, gave the same lame talks during Sacrament meeting, told the same faith-promoting urban legends.

It was supposed to be comforting that the Church had a uniformity everywhere you went, yet Cliff found it oddly disturbing that all the members he ever met were alike. He'd had three Jewish friends over the years, and they all believed different things. Their diversity hadn't harmed the Jews, who were part of what was surely one of the world's most enduring religions.

On his travels since, Cliff had tried to find comfort in the sameness of every ward he ever visited, but when he saw the remake of *The Stepford Wives*, he'd felt strangely uneasy. Mormons weren't programmed robots, he told himself. They were encouraged to study and pray and seek to know the truth for themselves.

Yet Cliff remembered how the Elders Quorum president a few years back had stood up in Fast and Testimony meeting. Most people who spoke during the monthly meeting seemed to be trying to convince themselves they believed and were happy, but this man stood in front of everyone and proclaimed that he had studied and prayed and been told by God that women should be allowed to hold the priesthood.

He'd been pulled aside afterward and told he was allowed to ask God these things, but he was only allowed to get the same answer the leaders gave. Anything else was apostasy and therefore unacceptable.

The Elders Quorum president had eventually been excommunicated. He continued to attend meetings, but no one talked to him anymore, afraid of being contaminated, as if he had some kind of viral infection that would turn them into evil monsters. In the end, the man had stopped coming to church.

"He felt too uncomfortable to be in our presence," the new Elders Quorum president said. "Sin will do that." Cliff had felt uncomfortable, too, but he quickly suppressed the thought.

"Okay, Dr. Ryan, give me a call if you have any more trouble."

"Sure thing, Brother Carlyle. Thanks a bunch."

Cliff walked out of the office, still irritated. The man was clearly brain damaged and would be calling again in a week or two. How did such a person ever get to be a full professor? How did he get to be a leader in the Church? How could any organization function with so many people blindly on autopilot?

Walking back to IT, Cliff passed several students in the hallway. One was a cute girl, probably a freshman. He smiled when he saw her but then stopped in his tracks when he read her T-shirt. "Be Happy. Be Mormon." He felt annoyed again.

Back in his office, Cliff did some paperwork. Then he was off another time to help an instructor with PowerPoint. Then he came back and played his computer game for a few minutes. After Cliff woke from his nap during lunch, Sandria came up to him and said, "It's time for us to start running our zombie check."

At first, Cliff thought she was referring to his game and felt confused. Then his head cleared as he became more awake. "I'll get right on it," he said.

The department periodically had to ensure that the university's computers were not zombies, hacked into and forced to perform unwanted tasks under remote direction. It happened all over the world, and with a network as large as theirs, the university was continually dealing with viruses or worms or zombieism or some other hassle.

Around 3:00, all the IT personnel gathered back in the office for "the announcement." They'd decided they wanted to do this communally rather than have Sandria approach the lone victim while he was isolated in his cubicle.

"The decision was difficult to make," Sandria began. "You're all good workers, all intelligent, all dedicated. I feel I'm friends with you all, and I didn't want to lose any of you. I had to take many things into consideration, and even then,

I don't feel justified in letting any of you go. But in the end, I still had to choose somebody."

Everyone waited breathlessly, except for Cliff. He hated paying his tithing when the family was always struggling, but he'd paid it again just last week, so he knew he was safe. Besides, he'd been here longer than half the others. Nevertheless, it would be good to finally hear the actual verdict. Sometimes, God did do mean things for no apparent reason.

"Cliff, we'll do everything we can to see that you find another job."

God *did* do it! Cliff couldn't believe it. And yet somehow, he realized he'd been expecting it all along. God took you out in the desert and then abandoned you. He made you prophet and then let you be murdered in jail. He ordered you to have a family and then left you in misery with them for the rest of your life.

Everyone quickly dispersed, and Cliff stalked back to his cubicle and started gathering his things. Then he grew suddenly angry and marched over to Sandria's office. "Dead man walking," someone muttered.

"Why me?" Cliff demanded, standing in the doorway.

"I had to pick someone," Sandria said slowly, "and you spend more time killing zombies than actually working."

"Everyone plays games."

"But you spend more time in a trance in front of your computer than anyone else. You don't have any intellectual curiosity. I had to find some deciding factor. Now be a good boy and leave on your own so I don't have to call security."

The words stung brutally for a moment, and then all feeling ceased. Cliff turned around in a daze and plodded back to his desk slowly. He felt dead inside. And yet, not that different than he normally did. He almost felt angry at that realization, too, but then felt nothing again.

How was he going to support his family now? How was he going to face everyone at church?

How was he going to face the rest of his life? He didn't think he could find another job in this economy. But he definitely didn't want to go back to school and learn something new. What was he to do?

Cliff knew that Sandria was right about his lack of intellectual curiosity. After beating himself into submission all his life, the only way he found he could make his spirit give in on so many issues was to force himself not to think at all anymore.

Well, he was going to think now. Jesuits thought, didn't they? And the Catholic Church survived just fine. It *benefited* from their thinking.

That would never work in his own culture, Cliff realized sadly. He was destined to a lifeless life. His family were destined to remain undead zombies for the rest of their lives, too.

Walking out to the car, Cliff had a sudden thought. The Church squashed people's souls, pretending to save them. It wasn't unlike a voodoo priest "rescuing" someone from the grave, only to force them into slavery for the rest of their lives. But Cliff could find a way to *really* save his family's souls. Jon hated Seminary. Liz hated being Homemaker instructor in Relief Society. The younger kids hated Primary. They were all as bad as he was. None of them was going to make it to the Celestial Kingdom, despite giving in all the time to the Church's demands.

But Cliff could guarantee them access to the highest kingdom. He could make them martyrs. One bullet to the head for each of them tonight would do it. They were already brain dead, weren't they? And he'd had plenty of practice shooting on the computer.

It was Friday, so no one would miss them until Monday. He could even go to church on Sunday and help redeem more of the zombies there as well, bring them all to Jesus. They thought that being a zombie was enough to get them to heaven. It wasn't, Cliff recognized now, but he would see that they made it anyway.

Cliff was finally going to do something genuinely useful with his life. Something legitimately righteous. He might go to hell himself, but that was a small price to pay for helping so many others. Was it even murder, to kill someone who was only half alive?

Cliff threw his box of belongings into the trunk of his car, feeling a lightness in his soul he hadn't felt in years.

He drove home carefully, thinking about where he'd stored his ammunition. If for some reason he decided he'd made a mistake, he could always ask God to raise his family from the dead like he'd raised Lazarus. If worse came to worst, they'd still all be raised from the grave during the resurrection. It would all be okay.

After parking carefully in the driveway, Cliff carried the garbage cans from the curb back to the house. Then he let himself in through the kitchen door. He saw Liz plodding listlessly across the floor toward him, and he smiled brightly for the first time in days.

"What's for dinner, hon?"

"Tuna casserole with lime Jello for dessert." Cliff laughed and gave Liz a peck on the lips, startling her. What a perfectly Mormon last meal, he thought. He sat in his easy chair and turned on the TV. Some stupid judge show was on.

Suddenly, a horrible thought struck Cliff. What if the resurrection on Judgment Day didn't bring people to eternal life but everyone was instead forced to continue to serve unhappily throughout eternity?

What if God really did want to make literal zombies of them all?

He sat there thinking furiously, and after a while, he realized with a shock that it was invigorating to be thinking so much. He was enjoying it.

Cliff looked to the kitchen, where Liz was still plodding slowly back and forth. Perhaps it was already too late to save anyone else, he reflected.

He'd have to think about himself for a change instead.

What did *he* want to do?

Cliff thought for a moment and then picked up the remote control. He flipped stations until he came upon the Discovery channel. There was a show on about African trypanosomiasis, sleeping sickness. Smiling, he sat back in his chair and watched as doctors talked about various treatments for the disease.

Maybe he could become a phlebotomist, Cliff thought. Or an X-ray tech. Something not too hard but which might still force him to think just a little. He could get a part-time job while he studied, and Liz could get a part-time job, too.

Jon burst through the kitchen door then and headed straight for his bedroom, but Cliff stopped him with a hand in the air.

"Yeah?"

"Just thought you ought to know you don't have to attend Seminary anymore."

Jon looked taken aback. "Really?"

"Really." He paused, wanting to say something more but not knowing what.

"You're not apostatizing, are you?" Jon laughed.

"Maybe I am," Cliff said carefully. "Would you have a problem with that?"

"Not if I can start seeing R-rated movies."

Cliff nodded. "I think it's about time. Pick something out and I'll go rent it for tonight."

"You mean it?"

"We'll have something for the other kids first, and after they're asleep, we'll stay up late and watch whatever you want."

"Hot damn!" Jon looked at Cliff guiltily. "Sorry."

"Curse all you goddamn want. Things are going to change around here."

"Are you feeling okay?"

"Just regaining consciousness after a coma."

Jon looked at him uncertainly. "You're acting kind of weird, Dad."

"That's *fucking* weird, Jon."

Jon smiled, still a little unsure. "Okay, Dad." He continued on to his room, and Cliff went back to his documentary.

He was coming back to life again after many years in the grave, and he felt good. This time, though, there'd be no voodoo, no sorcerer to control his actions.

"You going to nap before dinner?" asked Liz, trudging into the room. "It'll be about half an hour."

"No," said Cliff. "No more napping. I'm off for a run."

Liz's eyes widened, and Cliff thought he saw a glimmer of life there, too. Perhaps she could be saved eventually as well. He gave her a kiss, surprising her again, and then headed out the front door at a brisk pace. He felt the fresh spring breeze on his cheeks and smelled the mimosa in the air. Wondering what wild, stimulating movie was in store for him that evening, he broke into a run.

The Bishop's Confession

Bishop Randolph hated being a bishop. Yes, it was prestigious, and it was nice to have the respect, but the truth was, he wasn't worthy, and the guilt was too much to live with. Even since he'd studied in France for a semester abroad sixteen years earlier, he'd loved coffee. It wasn't the caffeine he was addicted to so much as the flavor. There were so many varieties, and he loved almost all of them.

With such Word of Wisdom problems, it had been hard to get a temple recommend so he could get married thirteen years ago. Keeping his recommend active all these years had been just as big a challenge. Bishop Randolph could go days or even weeks, sometimes a month or more, without coffee, but at some point, there would be an especially stressful day, and he would succumb.

Coffee was simply too wonderful to pass up every single day of your entire life. It worried the bishop that this indicated he'd never be happy in the Celestial Kingdom even if he did manage to make it there. An eternity without coffee? Was he cut out for that?

Resisting had been hard enough even before he became bishop eight months ago, but now, with all the added stress, it had become a nightmare. It was all he thought about at work. And on the weeks he faltered, what was he supposed to do on Sunday? He couldn't very well abstain from partaking of the Sacrament. How would that look? So he just tried to see the stake president regularly and confess.

Lately, though, the stake president seemed to be demonstrating less patience with his weakness. "You're supposed to be an example, Ted. This commandment is designed for the 'weakest of all saints.' You've got to put this behind you."

So the bishop kept praying and fasting and trying just a little bit harder every day.

Today was Sunday, and he'd had an entire week without coffee. Of course, after a 7:00 a.m. planning meeting this morning before the three hours of services began, Bishop Randolph was feeling more and more that one little cup wouldn't be so bad.

Bishop Randolph was tired, but now that services were over, he had two hours of interviews to do. Every Sunday was simply pure hell. "Good afternoon, Brother Taylor," the bishop said, welcoming a man in his mid-forties into the office. "What can I do for you today?"

They chit chatted for a couple of minutes before Brother Taylor was able to relax and open up. "Some guys at work the other day told a really dirty joke, and I laughed at it. I didn't walk away or tell them it was inappropriate or anything. I just laughed."

"I see." The bishop nodded his head thoughtfully. "Well, what's done is done. But what do you think you could do differently the next time such a situation arises?"

A teenage girl, a Laurel, was next, and she wrung her hands over the fact that two days earlier, she'd received too much change back at the store and kept it. Now she was afraid of getting the cashier in trouble if she brought the money back so late.

After this came a young returned missionary who couldn't keep from looking at women's breasts. He'd been caught staring twice this week. "Do you fantasize about women later and masturbate?" the bishop asked.

"Of course."

"Masturbation is a sin, you know, even if it *is* rather common among young adults."

"I'm just trying not to have sex. I'm not willing to give up whatever poor substitute I may have."

"Okay, but just try to sing a Church hymn when you get the urge, and see if that helps."

"All right, Bishop."

Another teenage girl came next, worried because her mother wasn't coming to church often enough, and then a fifteen-year-old boy being interviewed to be ordained as a priest next month guiltily confessed he'd tried a cigarette a couple of weeks before.

"Believe me, nothing good comes from smoking," the bishop said. "It costs a ton of money, makes you too winded to climb stairs, and gives you cancer. There are other ways to be cool."

"I guess."

"So tell me, Jim, do you have any problems with masturbation?"

The leaders were really trying to crack down on self-abuse. It so often seemed a precursor to even worse sins. Talking about it was terribly dreary, though. Bishop Randolph felt that almost everyone seemed to indulge in this unseemly practice. Even he'd done it as a teen, but he'd learned to control himself on his mission, and he'd been good about it ever since. Even now, only having sex with Maureen once a week, he was able to control himself.

He smiled. He could control himself sexually, but the mere smell of coffee sent him over the edge. It was pretty pathetic. Still, he sincerely wanted to help the members of his ward lead better lives, and if he could help even just a few of the members make honest improvements, that would be something to be proud of.

Jim looked down at the floor.

"Yes, Jim?"

"Bishop, do—do we have to talk about this? It's embarrassing."

"All sin will be shouted from the rooftops on Judgment Day. It's better to stop sinning now and not be embarrassed in front of the entire world later."

Jim was still looking at the floor.

"How often, Jim?" asked the bishop gently.

"I dunno. Maybe three times a week."

"There! You see? Some boys do it every single day. There's real hope for you. I know this is uncomfortable to discuss, but what are your triggers? What makes you start fondling yourself?" At times, simply just talking about it with underage boys made Bishop Randolph feel like a child molester. But this was for the boy's own good.

Even with Jim's face looking downward, the bishop could still see him turning red. "I dunno," said the boy. "Sometimes, I just wake up in the night and…you know."

"Jim, that's even more good news. It means that while you're awake, you're in control of yourself. There are a great many boys who would be lucky to say that." He thought for a moment. "So if it's just in the middle of the night, I wonder…"

Bishop Randolph was quiet for another moment, and Jim shifted uncomfortably in his seat. "Jim, would it be possible for you to tie one hand to the bedpost before you go to sleep?"

Jim looked up at that, a little puzzled. "I guess so. Why?"

"Then you won't be as likely to touch yourself in your sleep."

"But—" Jim turned red a second time and looked at the floor again.

"What, Jim?"

"It's just that, well, I only *need* one free hand, if you know what I mean."

The bishop nodded. "I see your point." He paused. "Do you think you could ask your father to tie both your hands to the bedposts?"

Jim looked at the bishop in alarm. "Oh, I could never! He'd know why I was asking!"

"I see." The bishop rubbed his chin. It was so hard to come up with effective strategies for avoiding sin. Coffee was ubiquitous at work, but at least at home, the bishop could avoid temptation. The boy's penis, however, was with him at all times. "What about your older brother Clay?" he suggested. "I know he doesn't come to church much anymore. We'll have to work on that. But do you think he'd be willing to help you out?"

"I dunno. We used to be pretty close. But lately he just looks at me funny and won't speak to me."

"Will you ask him?"

"I...I'll think about it." Jim looked at his watch nervously. "Look, my Mom is waiting. If we take too long, she'll think..."

"All right. But let's talk again next Sunday and see how you're doing."

Just a couple more interviews, thought Bishop Randolph, and he'd be free for the day. He'd never realized how taxing it was to hear all the sins and worries and pettiness and hurts of so many people. Hearing each confession was like dying a little. Some days, he wanted to give up on the whole human race. And this was simply hearing from Mormons, who were perhaps the most righteous of all people.

What must it be like for God, who heard all those prayers from millions of people of all religions, and saw everything even people who weren't praying were doing? Did he *really* want to become a god himself one day, the bishop wondered.

Soon Bishop Randolph was home, and he always made a point of playing Scrabble with the family after dinner on Sundays. Maureen had an English degree and worked as a substitute teacher. Kelly was twelve and a good student, so she liked to play. Scott was ten and would much rather play football, but the bishop forbade it on Sunday.

They were good kids, but on Kelly's next birthday, she'd officially be a teenager, and Bishop Randolph wasn't much looking forward to the next few years.

On Monday, Bishop Randolph was back at work. He was a supervisor with Metro public transit. He'd always liked his job well enough. But since becoming bishop, he started seeing things in a new light. When a customer complained that a bus driver skipped her stop, or someone complained that a driver wouldn't make the bus "kneel" for him, when someone complained that the driver allowed some teenagers to play music too loudly, he felt he was back in the confessional. Complaints were confessions from the other end, but they were still confessions. He still saw the moral fragility of other people every day.

Today's biggest complaint was that one bus driver kept honking and yelling at other drivers all along his route. It wasn't the first time people had complained about Mario. The bishop would have to talk to him again.

As the day wore on, Bishop Randolph kept finding reasons to walk past the coffee pot. He resisted drinking, but it was a close call. The bishop wanted to give himself a treat every time he resisted, but the only treat he really wanted was a cup of coffee.

Family Home Evening that night went well. Maureen talked about how cleanliness was next to godliness, and after thanking the kids for their help in keeping the house clean, she mentioned that Sister Bradley was sick, and they'd have to clean her house for the next week or two.

Scott rolled his eyes, but Bishop Randolph was pleased to see that this was the extent of the protest. Once the hormones started flowing in a couple of years, though, would his kids still be good? Hormones seemed to produce most of the world's misery. Sex, obviously, but even just plain old aggression and fighting were triggered by hormones.

If so much of the impulse to do evil was hormonal, Bishop Randolph wondered what percentage of responsibility the individual himself carried. Maybe a man was only 45% responsible for getting in a fight, only 23% responsible for fantasizing, only 11% responsible for making an irritable comment.

But hormones played no role in his desire for coffee. He was 100% on his own for that.

Work again was challenging on Tuesday. One of the drivers got in a minor accident but would still have to be drug-tested. Bill had tested positive for pot one time years ago, swore it was because of eating poppy seeds, and had passed all his screenings since. Was he cheating?

Wouldn't it be nice if there were some kind of test to show any of a hundred sins? Then the bishop wouldn't have to talk to his congregation, or at least, wouldn't have to listen to them.

At church that night, after a meeting with his counselors about Home Teaching statistics, he had two more interviews. "Bishop, I hit my wife," said a man about thirty, one of the outspoken men from the Elders Quorum.

"Why did you do that?"

"She always overcooks the broccoli. She knows I hate that."

"Is that worth hitting someone over?"

"It's the principle, Bishop. She isn't showing me respect."

"This is inappropriate behavior, Kevin. What can we do to help you control your impulses? Can you substitute hitting a pillow or taking a long walk?" Kevin resisted accepting a counseling referral but promised to report back to the bishop the following Sunday.

The next member was worse. Brother Tennant hemmed and hawed for almost fifteen minutes before the bishop could elicit the real reason for the visit. "I'm attracted to my daughter."

"Julia?" The bishop thought quickly. The girl was about thirteen.

Brother Tennant nodded. "I haven't done anything, of course. I wouldn't. But I think about it, and that makes me sick."

Bishop Randolph sighed. There was so much wickedness in the world. Brother Tennant had just been ordained a high priest not two months ago. And now this. "I'm going to recommend you see a counselor at LDS Social Services. If your insurance won't pay, we'll work something out."

"This is going on my record?" Brother Tennant looked aghast.

"A visit to a therapist will look a lot better on your record than a five-year-sentence at the penitentiary."

Brother Tennant nodded sadly, and they made the arrangements.

When he got home, the bishop went straight to bed. Maureen tried to engage him in conversation, but he just wasn't in the mood. Some 100% decaf coffee right now would be just perfect, he thought. He chewed on his pillow until he fell asleep.

Wednesday produced more trouble at work. Linda and Kim got into it. "You wear too much perfume," Linda complained. "You smell like a whore."

"I wouldn't know. I don't associate with whores. But you've got too much B.O. You shouldn't talk."

"I'm allergic to perfume. I've already reported it. If you keep wearing it, I'll bring disciplinary action."

"I *have* to wear perfume to keep from gagging every time you walk by smelling like a pig."

"I wouldn't know. I don't associate with pigs."

Bishop Randolph just stared longingly at the coffee pot.

Wednesday night after dinner, the bishop was back at church. The teenagers had an activity night, and the Single Adults were playing volleyball. Bishop Randolph saw Jim in the hallway and nodded, but the boy was with friends and pretended not to see him.

Karen, a young Single Adult about twenty-two, came to the bishop's office to talk. "My boyfriend's not a member," she said, "so he doesn't understand why I can't have sex." She hesitated. "He gets so impatient that I have to let him, you know, do it against me with his clothes on. That seems like a fair compromise, don't you think? A decent substitute?"

"Karen, you can't compromise at all with gospel principles. Something is either wrong or right."

"But he's such a good man. I'm sure I can convert him if we just go out a little longer."

"He'll never feel the Spirit while he's sinning, and you're helping him to sin."

"He's sinning less with me than if he was seeing someone else. *All* non-members are sinners, and hundreds of thousands of them still feel the Spirit enough to be baptized every year."

"You're rationalizing, Karen. You probably need to stop seeing this boy until after he gets baptized. If you tell him that, you'll see if he's serious about you or not. There's no substitute for true love."

Bishop Randolph wondered if the man's simply being baptized would change anything. The bishop was seeing every day that Church members were every bit as sinful as non-members. The idea saddened him, and he let out a deep sigh, drawing a worried look from Karen.

Maybe Jim, he thought. If he could just save Jim, he'd know he was a good bishop. He'd know he'd been forgiven about the coffee. He'd know he'd made a difference in the world.

Thursday at work, there were two major accidents in the city requiring the rerouting of two buses. There was road work in another location requiring yet another back-up route. And at a designated shift change, the relief driver for one line never showed up, and Bishop Randolph had one very tired, very angry bus driver on his hands.

That night was a miniature family night. The bishop had so little time with his family that he made sure to steal time for them whenever he could. Tonight they watched the Pixar movie *Up*. He liked kids' movies that were mature enough not to be insufferable for adults. He was sure that kept kids interested longer, too. Kelly and Scott seemed to enjoy the DVD, and Maureen did, too.

Bishop Randolph couldn't help but feel a little sad, though, when the childhood hero turned out to be a villain.

But maybe it was good to prepare children for that inevitable fact of life.

The bishop looked over at the kids. How long could he keep them pure? Kelly almost had an adult body already.

He watched the closing credits showing the happy boy and happy old man, and when Maureen smiled at him, the bishop smiled weakly back.

Friday was another nightmare at work. A car had run over a bus sign and several people complained that the bus had passed them right up. Didn't the drivers know their own routes? What was taking the company so long to put the sign back up?

Another woman complained that a bus driver had deliberately splashed her, and then several people complained when a driver accidentally took the wrong exit and delayed everyone by twenty minutes before being able to turn around and get back to his original route.

At 1:35, Bishop Randolph had a cup of coffee.

It felt so good, so incredibly soothing going down that he had a second cup. Then he locked himself inside a bathroom cubicle and tried to force himself to pee it all out, but of course it wouldn't come. He'd almost made it a whole week, and now he'd have to talk to the stake president again.

It would be humiliating to be released from his calling as bishop, but maybe that would be a blessing as well. He just had to help one of the other members before he left the position, though. Maybe Jim. The boy was still mostly innocent, still salvageable. He sure hoped he could help Jim.

Friday night, Bishop Randolph only spent an hour at church. He had to interview Brother Clarkson to talk him into paying tithing. He failed and couldn't help but suspect that the reason was simply that the Holy Ghost couldn't use him to bear witness because of his sin earlier in the day.

The bishop also had to interview a couple who were planning to be baptized the following day. They were about thirty, had one young child, and seemed nice enough. Bishop Randolph didn't press too hard, though. He didn't want to know their secrets.

He unfortunately did hear the secret the next man had. Brother Jeppson was a former Elders Quorum president with three children. "I look at porn almost every day. My wife is so fat, I can't help it."

"When was the first time you ever looked at pornography?" the bishop asked slowly.

"When I was twelve."

"And have you never looked at it again since then, till your wife got fat?"

"Well, no. Occasionally, I'd look. But now…"

"You shouldn't use your wife as an excuse, Brother Jeppson. Take responsibility for your own impulses. Don't use your wife as a substitute."

"I—I suppose you're right. But what am I to do?"

"Play sex games with your wife. Help her feel more attractive. She's probably embarrassed to be too sexual around you. Try to enjoy each other without judgment."

"I don't know, Bishop."

"There's a lot of sexuality that *is* allowed us. We just have to act within that framework."

"I'll try, Bishop."

"You know, in Polynesia, heavy women are often seen as sex objects. And you know that the painter Reubens was obsessed with heavy women. Most of his sexual paintings are about them. It's all in the way we look at things. If you think a thing is bad, then it is, regardless of the objective value of it. But whether or not being heavy is good, that's what you have to deal with, so it would be best if you could learn to like it. Others do, so you can, too."

You can learn to *like* paying tithing, he wanted to say. You can learn to *enjoy* ten hours of General Conference in one weekend. You can learn to *love* home teaching. He forced a smile onto his face, feeling like the fraud he was.

Brother Jeppson left, looking unconvinced, and Bishop Randolph stared at his desk for ten minutes before getting up.

Back at home, the bishop had to deal with Scott, who'd gotten into a fight with another boy after school. Scott refused to say what it was over, and the bishop wasn't sure it mattered. He took away Scott's Nintendo and went to his bedroom to pray.

Saturday morning, Bishop Randolph slept in till 7:45. Then he had some toast with a glass of orange juice and headed over to the church. There was a work party today, involving the Elders Quorum, the High Priests group, and the teenagers of the Young Men's program. They trimmed the hedges all over the church grounds and bagged all the clippings. Then they weeded the flowers.

Most of the others left before the work was completed, but Bishop Randolph stayed. It felt incredibly good to deal with something clear cut. He felt wholesome again.

He went home to change and then came back for the 1:00 baptism. Presiding over that was so energizing, so hopeful. Maybe there really was a point to all of this.

There was just one interview after the baptismal service. Sister Ramsey knocked on the bishop's door nervously. "I think my daughter may be using drugs," she said worriedly. "Her grades have gone down, and she is so moody lately. I looked in her purse and found a red pill, and when I asked her what it was, she laughed and said it was a Tic Tac. But what do I know? I'm not going to eat it to find out."

"Just let her know you love her, and try to find some things she likes to do that you can do as a family."

"She hates us."

"I'm sure that's not true. You just need to find something she really likes and share that with her. Not buying clothes. Teenage girls like to do that with other teenage girls. But she must like Taco Bell, or shopping for posters, or going to the library…"

"Going to the library?"

"Or something. You know your daughter better than I do. You have to show her that being with family is more fun than being with other people. And the only way you can do that is to *make* being with family fun. She has to learn to see her family in a new light."

They talked a while longer, but the bishop was pretty sure that if the girl really were taking drugs, she was already a lost soul. Her ability to see her family anew was probably no longer an option.

Wasn't the gospel supposed to help people lead better lives? Sure, there was temptation to face in life, but why wasn't the gospel strong enough to stand up to it? Why was everyone so bad? Even now, all the bishop himself could think of was sneaking in another cup of coffee before he had to talk to the stake president the next day.

Why was there so much human frailty? Could even the Atonement really make up for all of this? Even if they were all forgiven, weren't they still all miserable, weak creatures who would continue to sin despite their forgiveness, or at the very least still *desire* to sin, throughout eternity?

Perhaps after millions or billions of years, they'd grow beyond that, but who wanted to suffer miserably for millions or billions of years, even if that was only a fraction of eternity?

What *good* was it to be in heaven if you still wanted your cocaine? What good was it to be with the angels if you still wanted to look at pornography? What good was it to be creating your own worlds if all you really wanted was a cup of coffee?

The Church taught that you had to overcome your weaknesses here in this life or they'd follow you on to the next. That was why you couldn't do anything about them after you died, before the Resurrection, because you had no body to temper. Your spirit would still have all those cravings, but without a body, you couldn't learn to suppress them.

But if you had a body now and still couldn't suppress them, what was going to be different after the Resurrection? You'd still have the same personality, the same spirit. Your body might be perfect, but you'd have the same weak, miserable soul you always had.

Bishop Randolph went home and tossed the football back and forth to Scott for half an hour. The boy wanted to play with his friends, though, so the bishop nodded and went back inside. He turned on some soothing music and sat in the living room with Maureen, but she was reading a book and turned the music off. He went in the bedroom and took a nap.

After dinner, Bishop Randolph watched a little TV with the family, and then he headed over to church to make an appearance at the youth dance. He saw Jim in the hallway. The boy looked nervous, but the bishop asked him if he still planned to stop by his office on Sunday afternoon. Jim nodded uncomfortably and hurried off.

Bishop Randolph sighed. If the boy were this nervous, he must still be masturbating. He was nevertheless a good kid, though, wasn't he? Did masturbating really change all that? Did having a cup of coffee really make you a terrible person? Was being a fat wife so awful? A little sin wasn't the end of the world. It just made you more human.

But Mormons weren't supposed to be human. "Be ye therefore perfect, even as your Father which is in heaven is perfect." Mormons were supposed to become gods.

Sometimes, the bishop wondered if people came to him for confession all the time just as a substitute for living.

Back at home, Bishop Randolph and Maureen made love. Then Maureen got up to make some hot chocolate and read some more. The bishop just lay in bed staring at the ceiling in the dim light streaming into the room from the street lamp outside.

Sunday morning began early as always with the planning meeting before services started. During Sacrament meeting, the bishop listened politely to the superficial talks about faith and prayer. After Priesthood meeting, he had one hour of interviews before he had to speak to the stake president himself.

One young woman confessed she'd been to see an R-rated movie. Another admitted she'd eaten a rum-flavored pastry. And a newlywed man tearfully opened up about the fact he was still masturbating, even though he now had a wife he could have legitimate sex with.

This just wasn't going to work. Bishop Randolph would have to use the coffee as an excuse, as a stand-in for his real reason, and ask the stake president to release him from his calling. Life was hard enough just seeing his own sins. It was unbearable to see everyone else's.

Finally, Jim knocked on the door and came in. It would have been nice to have had at least one victory before leaving office, Bishop Randolph thought sadly.

"How are you today, Jim?" the bishop asked with forced cheerfulness.

"I—I think I'm in love."

The bishop was startled. This threw things into a new light. Was he going to have to worry about heavy petting now, too? Or actual intercourse?

"Whoa. One step at a time. Let's talk about what we discussed last week first. Did you try having your hands tied at night? Did your brother help you?"

"Well…"

"Jim, I'm your friend. We can talk openly. Did you masturbate this week?"

"Not exactly." The boy squirmed in his seat.

"Did you *kind of* masturbate?"

Jim shrugged. "Last Sunday night, I asked Clay to tie my hands to the bedposts, like you said. But then…"

"Yes?"

"After he tied me up, he kept looking at me. He looked and looked, and then…"

"What happened?" The bishop's stomach was sinking.

"He tied my T-shirt around my mouth."

"Oh my heck."

"Then…then we had sex." He paused. "We've done it every night this week." The boy looked at the bishop imploringly. "It's okay, isn't it? We're brothers. We're already sealed to each other in the temple. It's okay if you're sealed, isn't it? I—I love him."

"You love him?" the bishop asked weakly.

"Yes, Bishop."

"Does he love you?" The bishop felt dizzy.

"Yes, Bishop." He looked up hopefully. "Does this mean he doesn't have to tie me up anymore?"

The bishop nodded in a daze. "Not unless you like it that way."

Jim giggled. The bishop stood up and put his hand on the boy's shoulder. "You can go now," he said softly. "But don't tell anyone else about this. Not the stake president. Not the next bishop. You understand?"

Jim frowned. "Okay."

They shook hands and the boy left the office. Bishop Randolph sat back down and stared at the desk. It was time to go see the stake president. The bishop considered just skipping out and heading straight for Starbucks, but he decided that would be rude. He walked down the hall and knocked on the president's door.

"Hi, Ted. How are you today?"

"I don't think I'm cut out to be a bishop, Ken."

"Nonsense."

"I want to be released."

The stake president was silent for a long moment. "Well, Ted, the truth is we don't have anyone else we could call right now. Do you think you could hang on for another year?"

"Another year?" The bishop's head felt foggy.

"Yes. Just a little while longer. The Lord needs you."

Bishop Randolph stared at the floor for a couple of minutes.

"Ted?"

"Sure, Ken, I can hang on."

"That's the spirit."

They shook hands, and the bishop walked slowly out to his car. He drove off the church grounds and headed right past Starbucks without stopping. He pulled into a Safeway parking lot and walked calmly into the store.

After a moment, the bishop found the right aisle and picked up a can of Folgers. He could smell the coffee beans everywhere on this aisle. He breathed deeply and smiled, and finally he headed for the cash register.

The next stop was Walgreens to buy a coffee pot, and then the bishop turned his car toward home.

Shark among the Whales

Miranda hurriedly packed her suitcase. The mayor had just announced a mandatory evacuation for New Orleans, stating that the hurricane bearing down on the city was "the mother of all storms." After that last horrible hurricane, Miranda wasn't taking any chances.

She laid her most expensive clothes on the bottom of the suitcase. She could never afford to replace them. And then she put all her scrubs on top, in case the city was destroyed and she had to get a job somewhere else.

Miranda's car wouldn't make it to Baton Rouge in ten hours of stop and go traffic, so she drove to the parish office building on Clearview. There she joined huge throngs of people, mostly black, and waited for a bus. She could tell the blacks were wondering what a white girl was doing evacuating with them.

"She looks rich," she heard one of them say. "What's she doing here?"

Of course, Miranda wasn't rich. She'd lost three jobs in the past year and a half, and she had unpaid payday loans out with three different companies. If only everyone at work wasn't so mean. She'd lost her last job at the end of probation, because they found out she had a lawsuit pending at her job before that. They'd technically fired her at that other hospital for moving some cookies a patient's family had donated to the nurse's station, but she knew it was really because of the head lice.

Still, she didn't think she could sue based on medical discrimination. She sued because they called her a slut. A slut! And she hadn't had sex in ten years!

Miranda was forty-seven now. She'd had a hysterectomy two years earlier and would never have children. It had been a huge blow, but just as big a blow had been when Keith had died of Lou Gehrig's disease. He'd been married to his second wife for twelve years by then, but Miranda had always believed he'd come back to her.

Even when he was limping on his cane, hardly able to walk, he'd come over and try to rip her clothes off. She'd insist they get married first, but he'd just laugh and masturbate while looking at her. She knew he really loved her.

But Keith was dead now and she was alone.

Miranda climbed aboard a bus with some other poor people, hoping her suitcase wouldn't get lost or stolen. A fat black man sat next to her, resting his hand halfway on her leg. But she was a little hefty herself and couldn't squeeze herself over any further into her seat.

Twenty-four hours on the bus. It was going to be hell.

But it wasn't twenty-four hours. They drove to the airport instead. They were going to fly the evacuees somewhere. Oh god, thought Miranda. Please, not Salt Lake City. What would she do among all those Mormons?

She remembered the Mormon doctor from the hospital. He'd been nice to her until the hysterectomy, when Miranda had been forced to go to church for the first time in twenty years, to get welfare money from the bishop until she was back on her feet.

Miranda had been sitting in the back of the chapel one day, crying softly over her loss, when she distinctly heard the bishop's wife whisper to the doctor's wife next to her, "The Lord didn't want someone like that having children." The doctor had been cool to her ever since.

But the police wouldn't tell the evacuees where they were going. They just herded the mass of people along. At security, the guards looked through her luggage, and when they saw the nice clothes on the bottom, one of them said, "She's just in this for the FEMA money."

But that wasn't the worst. She heard a police officer tell a Red Cross worker standing next to the line, "Be careful. She's got head lice."

That proved the police were stalking her. As if she needed any more proof. One of the nurses who hated her, two hospitals ago, had been dating a police officer, and ever since, Miranda had seen police cruisers circling her apartment building, and overheard officers talking about her when she ran into them in convenience stores.

"That's the girl," she heard one of them say once as she walked past them near a casino on the lakefront. "That's the home wrecker."

It just made her so mad. She hadn't actually dated either the Arab doctor or the Jewish one. She'd just been nice to them both because they'd been nice to her. Was that so wrong? She wasn't trying to break up their families. It would have been different if they'd decided to divorce on their own and then start dating her. But she was no home wrecker!

Once on the plane, Miranda found herself sitting next to another fat black man. He kept leaning onto Miranda, pretending he simply wanted to see out the window, but Miranda wasn't fooled. She knew what was going on. But there was nothing she could do. Maybe she should tell him she had head lice. People said blacks didn't get lice, but she knew they did.

"Okay, folks, now that we're in the air, we can tell you you're on your way to Louisville, Kentucky."

There was a mixed rumbling of both approval and disapproval. Miranda didn't really care where she went, as long as it was far away. She'd brought her resumé with her. If Louisville looked okay, she might just look for a job there and get a fresh start.

Hospitals were so incestuous in New Orleans. Every time she was driven from one place to another, someone at the new hospital would have a friend from the other and the rumors would transfer along with her.

As New Orleans faded away behind her, Miranda realized she was like Lehi in the Book of Mormon, having left her homeland to escape the impending destruction coming to punish the unrepentant sinners, like those nurses who stayed behind. The other evacuees with her, though, were like Laman and Lemuel, unbelievers who'd been forced out with the good but who would bring a terrible storm sometime later along the voyage.

A few hours later, they were at the Louisville airport, and as the bus took her to the convention center, she noticed how clean the city looked, very different from New Orleans. Soon she was set up on a cot along with 2000 other people, almost all of them black. A cute guy in dreadlocks started putting his things on the cot next to Miranda, but a Red Cross worker came over and told him, "We're trying to keep the single men separated from the single women."

The man rolled his eyes and looked at Miranda with a smile. She smiled back, just to be nice, but then she overheard the Red Cross worker whisper, "She has head lice," and the man picked up his things and moved away.

Miranda didn't care. She didn't like men with dreadlocks, anyway. She sat on her cot for a while but then began feeling antsy, so she got up to walk around. On the far end of the room, she heard two women arguing.

She was going to steer around the fracas, but as she got closer, she could overhear that the women were arguing about religion. Then, to her amazement, she realized it was a Mormon woman arguing with a Jehovah's Witness.

Miranda wasn't at all sure she still believed in the Church, but it was exciting seeing someone else who did. Maybe it would be like in the Book of Mormon when Ammon and the Lamanite king fell down prostrate, and Miranda could go around like the secret Lamanite convert woman Abish and gather everyone together and have them all witness a miracle.

The Church always looked down on her. But she might bring a thousand converts to baptism now. Men in the Church would start wanting to be around her again. Miranda watched the argument progress, her heart pounding as she waited for them to be overcome by the power of the Spirit. The hurricane was simply God's way of bringing all these other people together to see this. Miranda was going to be famous in the Church. And she was going to have a prominent Mormon husband.

The Jehovah's Witness snapped her Bible shut in the Mormon woman's face, and Miranda could see the Mormon woman was livid. Cut her, cut her, Miranda urged the woman in her mind. Make her need a transfusion and then let God heal her.

But the Mormon woman just turned on her heels and walked off.

Just like a Mormon, Miranda thought in disgust. Always wimps. That's why they didn't like her. Because she stood up for herself. Mormons didn't approve of strong women like her.

But they'd like her when she had money, when she won her lawsuit. They'd want her tithing. She smiled as she thought about the bishop being nice to her for a change. She'd make the bishop's wife be nice to her, too.

Miranda was exhausted after a twelve-hour shift at work followed by staying up listening to the news reports and then packing and flying. It was still early, but she lay down on her cot and went right to sleep.

In the middle of the night, though, she heard a woman one cot over yelling. "I can't breathe! I can't breathe!"

She sure had a lot of lung power for someone with no breath, thought Miranda. A Red Cross worker came over and gave the woman some nose spray, and things settled down again.

The next morning, breakfast was served, and Miranda wolfed it down. She'd missed dinner the night before. Of course, she could stand to lose forty pounds, so it was no great loss. But now her hair was a mess, and she had no make-up. She must look a horror.

"Is there anything you need?" a Red Cross worker asked, moving from person to person.

"I could use a blow dryer," Miranda said. The people near her snickered.

Some buses came shortly after breakfast and took everyone to the amusement park, where they were given free admission. But rides always made Miranda queasy, so she just walked around and looked at everything. It was too hard to really enjoy her "vacation," though, knowing she wasn't getting paid for these days off. Sitting on a bench enjoying the breeze, she overheard two black people talking next to her. "Look at her posing, trying to get a man." Miranda stood up and walked away.

The next day, Miranda discovered that the Red Cross had divided everyone into groups. Miranda laughed when she heard the names. There were the whales, and sure enough, the group consisted of people who just lay around on their cots all day. Then there were the parrots, the people who kept talking and talking all day and half the night. There were also the antelopes, the people who ran around and played ball all day.

But Miranda was upset to discover she'd been grouped with the sharks. These were the anti-social people who just wandered around on their own and only showed up for meals. She was a little put out by the label, but she realized she didn't want to belong to any of the other categories, either. Why couldn't there be a group of butterflies? Or hummingbirds? Or something else nice?

Today, everyone who wanted to go was bused to the Mohamed Ali museum. The blacks loved it, and Miranda had to admit, it was pretty impressive.

Back at the convention center, she learned that the hurricane had missed New Orleans and struck central Louisiana, but there was still some damage in the city, some power outages, and people weren't allowed to return just yet.

While she was eating dinner, Miranda heard two of the Red Cross workers talking about her. "Look how much she eats!"

Why would they say such a thing? Miranda fumed as she walked back to her cot. It wasn't as if she served herself. She was given a plate like everyone else, with no more food and no less on her plate than on any other. Why were people always so mean to her?

That night around 3:00, Miranda woke up when the woman beside her began yelling. "I need a glass of water! I need a glass of water!"

The woman wasn't a cripple. Why didn't she just get up and get some water herself? Sheesh.

In the morning, Miranda took a shower. The Red Cross had set up some good showers, but there were several women who didn't want to use them, choosing instead to bathe in the sinks where everyone had to brush their teeth. And they bathed their feces-covered babies there, too. There was always hair left all over the sinks and counters. It was repulsive.

But today, the group was given free admission to the science museum. The place was mostly geared toward children, but it was still pretty interesting.

Miranda was getting bored, though. She wished she could go back to work, even if the other nurses made her life hell. She was only a nursing secretary, since she'd flunked out of nursing school, but the nurses always seemed to feel she was a threat anyway.

When a cute doctor had come up to talk to her once, one of the nurses deliberately blocked his path and told him, "She's nothing but trouble. Stay away from her."

Miranda knew the nurses were afraid she'd marry a doctor. The doctors liked her because she was smart and funny and efficient. And really, despite the weight, she had a pretty face and a pretty voice, and she could tell more men looked at her breasts than at her pudgy stomach.

The Arab doctor had even invited her on a riverboat cruise, but one of the nurses overheard, and Miranda saw her run off to tell the other nurses. The next day, "mysteriously," the doctor changed his mind and invited a woman doctor instead. Miranda wasn't stupid, though. She knew the nurses had turned him against her.

The woman doctor was also Arabic, and she lived in Miranda's apartment complex. And one day when Miranda went to get her mail, she overheard two of her neighbors talking. "*She* thinks she can get *him*? Not with those pictures going around."

The apartment complex had just done major remodeling on everyone's apartment, enclosing the outdoor balconies into sunrooms. Miranda had suspected the workers might have installed spy cameras in her apartment and now she knew.

There were pictures of her floating around on the internet! She already knew the police had tapped her phone. She could hear the clicks when she picked it up. But she obviously couldn't go to the police about any of this, so she went to the FBI.

She told her story, and the agent sounded sympathetic, but when he took her driver's license to make a copy, he gasped, though he tried to cover it up by faking a cough. And the very next day at Walmart, Miranda saw one of the women she'd seen in the FBI office. She got close enough to overhear her talking on her cell phone. "Anyone who looks like that is a loser!" she heard the woman say.

So the FBI wasn't going to help her because she took a bad driver's license picture!

Miranda had felt distraught. There simply had to be some justice in the world. The Church claimed to be the repository of truth and righteousness, so she went back to church and talked to the Mormon doctor she'd worked with before.

"You need to drop the lawsuit," he told her. "No one likes a troublemaker. No one is going to hire you again."

"I won't need them to. This is a multi-million dollar lawsuit. It's sexual harassment."

"I'd be careful if I were you. You're stressing yourself out too much. You know, one of our members just committed suicide a couple of weeks ago. She drowned herself. She was found dead in her car."

Miranda was floored. He was actually threatening her life. He knew she walked along the lake every day for exercise. He was threatening that she'd be found dead one day. He was obviously hinting pretty openly, too. How could someone drown herself and then walk back to her car? Was the Church after her money? Did they think she was going to win the lawsuit? Was that what this was all about?

Miranda needed to find a job here in Louisville, get a brand new start. Of course, she thought every time she moved to a new hospital in New Orleans it would be a brand new start. And what if another nurse from back home had evacuated to Louisville, too? What if she was getting a job here as well? Oh my god. Could she *never* get away from those horrible, horrible people? It wasn't fair.

That evening, she saw that the storm had moved into Arkansas and was causing flooding there. She hoped she could get back home soon. She was going to win that lawsuit and move far, far away.

Miranda felt restless, so she took another stroll around the auditorium. There were a few Hispanics, a few white trash people, no Asians, and hordes of blacks. Almost everyone looked pretty uneducated, and missing teeth seemed to be a common theme. Most people came in family groups, it appeared, but one old black woman sat alone knitting. She'd evacuated with her knitting needles.

Miranda smiled and debated over whether to talk to the woman. She remembered the passage, "Wherefore ye have done it unto one of the least of these my brethren, ye have done it unto me."

It was a sexist scripture, of course. Did it only count if you were nice to poor men, "brethren," and not women? Men always seemed to get the real breaks in life. Women fought each other over the scraps.

So Miranda walked up to the woman. "What are you knitting?" she asked softly.

"Baby blankets," the woman replied, not looking up. "I donate them to Goodwill."

"How sweet."

"You need to think of others first."

Miranda frowned. What did the woman mean by that? Had someone told her about the lawsuit? Did she think Miranda was being selfish to sue? What did that old woman know? She'd never been abused as Miranda had.

"Do *you* always think of others?" Miranda asked a little coldly.

"When you're all alone in the world, there's nothing else you can do, is there?"

And what did the woman mean by *that*? How did she know Miranda had no family? She was being awfully cheeky.

But she'd make one more attempt to be Christ-like. "Do you have a favorite color you like to knit?"

"All the colors of the rainbow. We need to remember God's promise after the Flood, especially in times like these. We can't forget God's goodness, no matter what happens." The woman gave Miranda a sharp look, and Miranda's mouth fell open.

Had someone told her about Miranda's miscarriage? How dare she accuse Miranda of forgetting about God? You tried to be nice to people and this was what you always got. Miranda turned around and walked off without a word.

The parrots and antelope kept her awake until late in the evening, but Miranda eventually fell asleep. In the middle of the night, though, the woman in the cot next to her began yelling again. "I have to pee! I have to pee!"

Miranda had just about had enough. She sat up and looked at the woman coldly. "I guess we'll have to get you a wheelchair if you can't get up and walk to the bathroom."

The woman shut up immediately. "I ain't going to no hospital!" She climbed out of the cot and walked off to the bathroom.

Miranda expected her neighbors would appreciate what she'd done, but she could hear one of them muttering, "What has she got against old black people?"

Miranda got up and walked toward her, but the woman started coughing. She did this every time Miranda got near her. Miranda knew the woman was simply trying to keep her away so she wouldn't catch her lice, but Miranda just fumed. What was worse? Getting head lice or getting tuberculosis? The woman had no reason to be so self-righteous.

Miranda took a walk around the auditorium. She stopped when she came upon the man with the dreadlocks. It would have been nice to have someone to talk to here.

A little girl was playing with a rubber ball, and Miranda watched her bounce it up and down. If she hadn't had that miscarriage…wait a minute. That was over twenty-five years ago. She could have a *granddaughter* this age by now. Miranda had always felt so maternal around children, but she didn't know what she should be feeling now.

She certainly didn't want to feel grandmotherly. If she won the lawsuit, she'd have enough money to adopt a child. Maybe two. She'd still get her time as a mother. She wouldn't be cheated forever. Life was still going to be good for her.

The girl dropped her ball, and it rolled under a cot where a skinny man with track marks on his arms was sleeping. The girl looked as if she wanted her ball but was too afraid to retrieve it.

Miranda smiled at her and got down on the floor and reached under the cot. A police officer started walking toward her, but Miranda stood up and offered the ball to the girl, who turned and ran away.

Miranda walked back to her cot and went back to sleep.

The next day, everyone was bused to Churchill Downs. Miranda had never been much of a gambler. She only bought lottery tickets a few times a year. She wasn't about to waste her time fantasizing about impossible dreams. The Church said gambling was a sin. But it was interesting to see the place.

She tried to memorize every detail so she could tell the Mormon doctor next time she saw him. She knew he'd disapprove, and that would be fun to watch. He'd be afraid she was going to lose all her money from the lawsuit, and the Church wouldn't get its cut. She smiled.

When she turned, she saw a TV camera in her face. Reporters had been following the evacuees around for days, showing everyone how nice the townspeople were being to them. Miranda had avoided being filmed, still upset about her hair. Her eyes grew big now and she twisted about and hurried off.

What if the EEOC back in New Orleans saw her looking like this? They'd drop her case. Had the hospital paid the reporters to follow her? She knew they'd paid off some of the doctors to testify against her. She'd overheard the charge nurse talking about it.

The nurses had also said she was white trash, that when they saw her shopping on her days off, she was dressed too nicely for what she made. She must be a hooker, they said. So she was dressed nicely, but she was white trash. They always contradicted themselves. But what would they say when they found out she'd gone to Kentucky? They'd start calling her a hillbilly hooker. How could they be so mean?

Well, it didn't matter. If they said anything, she'd sue this hospital, too. There was no reason she couldn't win two lawsuits.

Back at the convention center, Miranda saw that the remains of the storm were in Missouri now. New Orleans had long since been spared. When would they ever get home? She couldn't go forever without a paycheck.

She wondered if she should start flirting with one of the police officers guarding the evacuees. She could move up here and get married. Oh, why couldn't they get her a blow dryer? She'd never evacuate again without one.

Miranda put on one of her nice outfits and walked around and around the auditorium. Sure enough, one of the police officers, an Italian-looking man about forty, not too young, started following her. She smiled. She still had it.

She never flirted at work. The nurses did it all the time, but she'd been told flat out she'd be fired if she flirted. But she wasn't at work now.

The officer positioned himself so Miranda would have to walk right past him. Miranda smiled sweetly and blushed a little.

"Ma'am?"

Miranda frowned. She still preferred "Miss," but it had been a long time since she'd heard that title directed toward her. She still felt like a "Miss" inside, though.

"Good evening," she said in her Marilyn Monroe voice.

"You don't look like you belong here," he told her.

"My car is in the shop," she lied, "so I had to join the rest of the refugees."

"I figured it was something like that." He smiled. "Or you were working on a paper." He chuckled now. "I studied psychology before I joined the department."

"Oh, that was one of my best subjects," Miranda said. "My only bad subject was math."

"I was no good at math, either. That's why I ended up on the force instead of being a psychologist." He smiled again, and Miranda did, too. This was a guy who could really understand her. She felt a little thrill run through her body.

They walked along together and talked for half an hour. It was Miranda's first date in how many years? Watching Keith masturbate didn't count.

Miranda saw the other people sitting on their cots pointing at her, but she didn't care. This guy had a full head of hair, and he was tall and good looking. He had everything she needed.

Finally, though, Miranda felt it was time to end the date. She'd read *The Rules*. She knew you were always supposed to leave the man wanting more. "I have to go to the bathroom now," she said. She obviously couldn't claim another commitment.

"Why don't you use the police officers' bathroom?" he suggested. "It'll be nicer."

Miranda smiled. He liked her. She followed him to the bathroom and went inside. Before she could get to the stall, however, she saw a huge sign posted over the sink. "Wash your hands after leaving the animal area. Stay healthy."

Miranda's mouth fell open. That was another lawsuit waiting to happen. She wished she had her cell phone with her so she could take a picture. Maybe she could get this guy to admit to other things like this. It wouldn't hurt to win two lawsuits. Or three, if she did go after that second hospital, too.

"How about tomorrow night I bring some take-out?" the officer asked when Miranda came out of the bathroom.

"That would be very nice," she said, smiling and lowering her eyes seductively.

She went back to her cot. The wheelchair lady glared at her, and the woman with TB coughed loudly in her direction. But Miranda smiled and pulled out a book to read. At least she'd been smart enough to bring some reading material along.

Miranda had a good night's sleep and had a fun time the next day at the Slugger bat museum with its huge bat towering over the building. When she walked next to two other women from the shelter, though, she heard one of them say to the other, "I hear she had sex in the bathroom."

Miranda couldn't believe it. Had the officer told everyone they'd had sex when she went in their bathroom? Men were such pigs. But she could take it. Keith had been a pig, too, and he'd even had the gall to marry someone else. Yet he'd kept seeing her up until two months before he died.

Once she married this guy, she didn't care what he said. As long as he loved her. And she could tell he was well on his way toward that.

Miranda put on one of her other nice outfits when she got back to the convention center. Around 7:00, she saw the officer walking toward her. She smiled and moved over to meet him.

"In the mood for chicken?" he asked with a grin.

What was that supposed to mean? Did he think she was too old for him?

"In Kentucky?" she said, laughing. "I guess it's the law here."

She wasn't happy about getting her hands all greasy. Eating fried chicken always seemed so undignified. But the dinner went well, thank goodness. Last night, the officer had talked about himself. Tonight, he asked about Miranda, and though she wanted to maintain a mysterious aura, she found herself telling him everything, in exhaustive detail. She enjoyed having a captive audience, and besides, if he thought she was about to win a big lawsuit, he might be more inclined to marry her.

Miranda could see the concern on his face as she talked, and it touched her. No one had cared what she thought for a very long while. Maybe she really was going to find happiness after all this time. She felt her heart beating a little quickly, and it beat even faster when the officer took her hand.

"Miranda," he said gently, "it's been a long time since I was in class…"

She frowned. Did he want to go back to college on her settlement money?

"But it's clear you need some help. I'm not sure if you have borderline personality disorder or schizophrenia or are just delusional, but you need to see a doctor. Hasn't anyone ever told you this before? You're going to end up fired again, and no one is going to hire you, and you'll be living in places like this the rest of your life. You've got to get some help."

Miranda's mouth fell open. What did he mean by borderline personality? She had a wonderful personality. Was he crazy? How could he blame all that had happened on her? Hadn't he been listening? Was he just trying to be mean? Was he simply looking for a way to break up?

Then it dawned on her. He was a police officer, wasn't he? The police back home had contacted him, obviously. They were still after her even from a thousand miles away. She should have known all along something was up when he'd pretended to be nice to her.

"I do have a disease," she said sadly. "It's called head lice."

The officer withdrew his hand, and Miranda smiled.

"You say you've had this at least two years. Most people use a medicated shampoo and they're fine the next day. At worst, it takes two shampoos. You don't have head lice. Some people with mental illnesses are convinced they're infected with maggots internally. It's the same thing."

Miranda stood up, horrified. "You didn't just feed me maggots in that chicken, did you?"

The officer looked at her solemnly for a long moment. Then he stood up. "Good luck, Miranda," he said and walked off.

Good luck? What did he mean by that? Had he really put something in her food? What if she died up here in Kentucky? No one would ever find her. No one would ever know what had happened. Was the Church behind this? Was it the hospital?

Miranda hurried to the bathroom and forced herself to throw up. She tried to look in the toilet to see if there were any maggots in the mess, but she couldn't tell. But she should be okay, she thought. If she wasn't, she'd sue. The Louisville police would sure be sorry they'd messed with her.

Miranda walked back to her cot. As she passed the woman with TB, the woman coughed at her, and Miranda coughed right back.

"Hey!"

Miranda smiled and began deliberately scratching her head, even though it didn't itch.

No one bothered her.

She slept soundly through most of the night, though she did wake up around 4:00 from her stomach growling. She felt the rumbles and wondered if that was just the gastric juices bubbling or if it were maggots crawling. Damn that officer.

After breakfast, Miranda felt better. Everyone was carted off to the zoo today, and Miranda especially liked looking at the antelope and the parrots. She laughed as she realized just how right the Red Cross had been.

But when she got back to the convention center, the officials were rounding everyone up. They were finally going back to New Orleans. Thank God. Of course, by this time, there was probably another hurricane on its way. Or at least regular bad weather. Miranda was so tired of all the heat and mosquitoes and thunderstorms and termites and roaches in New Orleans.

But maybe she'd meet a cute male flight attendant who had an apartment in another state. He'd see her on the plane and realize she didn't belong in this crowd and start talking to her and they'd start a romance in the air. She felt a thrill as she thought about it.

It was several more hours before Miranda's group boarded the bus. A cute man in his late thirties sat next to her, and he looked at her kindly and had nice smile lines on his face. Maybe she was going to have two romances on the flight. She was still desirable. That's why the other nurses didn't like her.

"I'm a whale," the man offered with a grin. "How about you?"

"A shark," Miranda said, snapping her jaws playfully.

They began talking, and it turned out that the man's mother had been a nurse as he was growing up. "But she died several years ago."

"My parents are both dead, too," said Miranda, "but I get along okay."

"You look like a woman who knows how to get what she wants out of life."

Miranda smiled. She hadn't even mentioned the lawsuit yet, so he couldn't be after her for her money.

Miranda managed to sit next to him on the plane, making it look like a coincidence. She laughed, and the man did, too.

He asked the flight attendant for a blanket and draped it over both their laps. It was nighttime by now, and the man turned off his overhead light and nodded for Miranda to do the same. She felt a little thrill and switched off her lamp. A moment later, she felt a hand on her leg.

She was a good girl, so she wouldn't do anything even after they were dating. But she smiled now in the dim light. The evacuation had been a blessing, after all. God sometimes seemed to have it in for her, but he was coming through for her now.

She put her hand on top of the man's hand and squeezed. He in turn squeezed her thigh, and he leaned over to kiss her. Miranda allowed a quick peck and then pulled away, not wanting him to get the wrong idea, but she was happy.

Miranda was finally going to have a man, and a settlement, and she was going to have money and time to join a gym and lose some weight. Those nurses would sure be jealous. They would boil in their own juices knowing it was their meanness that had made it all possible. And she couldn't wait till she could walk back in the chapel and sit next to the Mormon doctor with a black man at her side.

Maybe when he saw that other guys were interested in her, he'd leave his bitch of a wife. And maybe when the bishop saw that the Mormon doctor wanted her, the bishop would want her, too. Miranda giggled.

The young man smiled at her in response and moved her hand under the blanket, placing it on his crotch. Typical. But he didn't unzip, so he was far more of a gentleman than Keith had ever been.

She caressed him gently in gratitude.

The plane headed down toward Miranda's new life. She sighed happily and drifted gently off to sleep, her hand still resting on her new boyfriend's hardened crotch. She dreamed of babies and balls and running horses, and she smiled a little in her sleep.

She dreamed of all the clothes she could buy with her winnings, and how she'd parade around in front of all the other nurses. She dreamed of her new car and her new two-story house. She dreamed of the doctors who would court her, and the beautiful children with caramel skin her handsome husband would bring to the marriage. She murmured dreamily, nuzzling against the man sitting beside her.

She vaguely sensed him reaching under her skirt and caressing her gently as well.

She slept on soundly till morning.

A Life of Their Own

"Dr. Taylor, my breasts feel funny." Sister Anderson was one of my patients who was also a member of my ward. Even as a busy plastic surgeon, I'd been called two years ago to be our ward's lay bishop. I'd devoted my life to fixing wrongs in the form of car accident scars and mastectomies, but the last two years I'd had to balance that with worrying about the spiritual wrongs my congregants were facing.

It created a kind of coexistence in my soul acting as both a physical and a spiritual healer. Jesus had done both, too, I reflected, so I was well on my way to becoming like him. My brother Theo certainly liked to crucify me whenever he had the chance.

"What do you mean, Valerie?" Sister Anderson liked to be called by her first name in my office. This always felt a little awkward, as she was the stake president's wife, and the stake president was a notch higher than I was, head over eight congregations while I presided over only one.

I'd put breast implants in Sister Anderson over a year ago due to stage two cancer. It was always exciting to turn a death sentence into a reason for living.

"I don't know. They—they tingle. You don't think they've burst? You don't suppose the cancer is back?" I'd seen hickeys on the necks of many teenagers over the years, but Sister Anderson was the only person I knew with hickeys on her breasts. I expected they tingled a lot.

"You're only one month away from your scheduled checkup. Let's go ahead and do some tests today."

We did the tests, but I was pretty sure the symptoms were all in Sister Anderson's mind. She was one of those Mormons who'd bought a generator in case all the world's computers stopped working in 2000. She had a year's supply of food stored underneath her stairwell.

Her husband made $70,000 annually, and yet she still sewed most of her own clothes. When doing her genealogy, she came across an ancestor's name in the family tree frontispiece of a novel she was reading and incorporated the history of the fictional family into her own family group sheets.

She was also one of those Mormons who was already half living in the afterlife. When I'd reconstructed her breasts, she told me she was worried about how this would affect her ability to bear spirit children later when she became a god and needed to nurse them. I assured her as her bishop that she'd be resurrected with her original breasts intact.

She asked if she could be resurrected with larger ones, for her husband's sake. I thought it might be better if he was simply resurrected with smaller hands, or a smaller mouth.

It would be unlikely, I thought, that Sister Anderson's gel implants had burst or begun leaking and causing some kind of connective tissue disorder. That had been only a minor problem even in the old days, before a moratorium on using them was imposed back in 1992. For the next fifteen years, women could only get this type of implant if they were part of a study, but since 2006, they were common practice again. The difference was that the bag they were in now was thicker and stronger. It made the implants feel a little less natural, but they were also pretty darn secure, no matter how rough President Anderson might be with them.

"When will the results be back, Bishop? I mean, Doctor?"

"You know how this works, Valerie. It'll be a couple of days. I'll give you a call."

"But the X-ray looks normal?"

I hesitated. Actually, the X-ray didn't look normal at all. In fact, it didn't look like anything I'd ever seen before. Not ruptured. Not cancerous. But not normal. I didn't want to say anything, though, until the other results were back. No sense worrying the poor woman for nothing.

"Let's reschedule you for a week from today, just in case we need to do something more. In all likelihood, I'll be giving you a call in a few days with an all clear, and we'll cancel the appointment, but it won't hurt to have some time set aside as a backup."

Naturally, if there were any sign of cancer, I'd send her back to her oncologist, but she'd come to me this time, and I could at least run these preliminary tests.

"You *do* think something's wrong."

"Let me just feel them one more time."

Sister Anderson always looked uncomfortable when I put my hands on her breasts. She seemed to think she was committing adultery. I wanted to reassure her that a doctor's physical exam was not a sexual act, but she seemed to need to feel extra righteous in a way that assumed all physical contact was forbidden, so I just lifted and pressed and felt in silence.

"Oh."

"What, Bishop? I mean, Doctor."

"Nothing."

"What?"

I laughed. "It's just that you moved. It made it feel like your breasts twitched."

"I didn't move."

I shrugged. I wasn't going to make a federal case of it.

Sister Anderson leaned forward and whispered. "They seem—they seem to have a life of their own." She looked around as if someone might be listening. "Some days, they're perky and some days they droop. And it has nothing at all to do with…with…you know."

I nodded. "I'm sure everything is fine. But I'll call you as soon as I know, one way or the other."

"All right."

"Any plans for the rest of the day?"

"I'm going to help my granddaughter sell Girl Scout cookies, and then I'll study for Gospel Doctrine. I like to know the answers for class on Sunday."

After she left, I stared at the X-ray for a long while.

I thought about why Sister Anderson had wanted breast implants in the first place. She was in her early fifties, married thirty years, and didn't need to look sexy any more. But as prudish as Mormons could be, we also had an odd streak of sexual obsession.

We believed if we were righteous enough in this life, we'd be rewarded a place in the Celestial Kingdom with our partner and enjoy a sexual relationship for eternity. Only the super righteous would reap this particular reward. All others would have celibacy enforced upon them throughout the eons.

But the gift of everlasting sex came with a price tag. We would have to create our own worlds and run those planets as our God ran ours. Obviously, we'd have to people the planets by having millions, even billions, of spiritual offspring who then went to the planets to gain physical bodies. And we'd also have to create the mountains and oceans and birds and maybe experiment first by creating our own dinosaurs and other creatures as well.

My wife Sally and I even discussed some of the animals we might like to create some day. People would always be people, of course, but we could play around a little with the animals. Sally was adamant about creating colored fur. She absolutely thought green fur would function as camouflage, but she insisted we try purple and red at least once to see how it might succeed.

"Birds and fish have all these brilliant colors. Why can't we try it with mammals, too?" She liked to talk about all kinds of different possibilities we could develop while populating our planets. Flying cats. Dogs with arms as well as legs. Flowers that could transplant themselves if they needed to find better soil conditions.

I, however, was mostly hoping that somehow once we were on the other side of the veil, sex would become a little more interesting, as it had been when we first got married. If it was sometimes stale now after only twenty years, what would it be like after a thousand? Ten thousand? A million?

At times, Sally and I pretended I was raping her, or that she was the prophet's wife, or a patient under anesthesia, or whatever else we could think of. It occasionally disturbed me I could get an erection even when Sally was pretending to be a corpse. Did gods play sex games to liven up the Celestial bedroom, too?

Even with the possibility of eternal polygamy, I wanted some promise of excitement or the blessing of sex might end up a curse. Was that why God so often seemed in a bad mood?

Still, if the alternative was everlasting celibacy, I was determined to be worthy of the Celestial Kingdom and not just the Terrestrial or, God forbid, the Telestial.

I called Sister Anderson on Friday. "There's no sign of cancer," I said simply, "and no suggestion of leakage, though we really can't be sure of that without doing something a little more invasive."

"Perhaps we'd better then."

"What's wrong?"

"Bishop Taylor, I mean, Doctor Taylor, I've—I've had—" She paused a long while. "My nipples have this crusty stuff on them now all the time. It was just a little bit before. I thought it was dirt at first, that I wasn't bathing well. But it's worse now. Oh, this is so embarrassing."

That sounded like an infection more than anything else, but Sister Anderson's white count had been normal.

"You were scheduled for Tuesday, but do you think you could come back in today?"

"Oh, thank you, Doctor."

Sister Anderson was at my office by noon, and I skipped lunch to squeeze her in. I took scrapings of the odd, gritty substance that seemed to be oozing from her nipples, and I prescribed an antibiotic. I palpated her breasts again, longer this time, once more feeling an odd twitch, and I scheduled an MRI for the following week.

"I'm sure it's just an infection," I said, "but the culture and the MRI will tell us more. I'll analyze this grit and call you when I know something. Your MRI is on Tuesday, so I'll cancel your appointment with me that day and have you come in Wednesday."

"I'll be okay by Wednesday, won't I?" Sister Anderson rubbed her nipple a little nervously. "Wednesdays and

Saturdays are the days Geoff and I—the days we—well, my husband likes to suck on them and…"

"You may have to do the sucking this next week."

"Oh, Bishop Taylor!"

I sent the scrapings to the lab right away, and before I left for the day, I had my answer. They were tiny nodules of silicon dioxide.

I was stumped. There was silicon in the grit, but silicon gel implants certainly weren't made of silicon dioxide, so I couldn't see how this might be related to a leak. Was Sister Anderson just playing with me, putting sand on her nipples and coming in so that I'd put my hands on her? Maybe this was her way of having an innocently illicit affair.

But her breasts had in fact felt funny, I remembered, and that X-ray was definitely odd. The MRI would tell me more, but I called up my brother Theo now.

"Victor? What's up?"

"Theo, I have a chemistry question for you." My brother was a professor at the university, the "smart" one in the family, though I earned four times as much even in a bad year.

"Sure. What do you have for me?"

"Well, you know silicone gel implants are just made out of silicone, right?"

"It's silicon mixed with oxygen, hydrogen, and carbon, yes. It's a middle molecular weight substance as a gel. If it were a low molecular weight, it would be an oil rather than a gel, and at a high molecular weight, it would be a rubber. You can do all kinds of things with silicon."

"Yeah, well." I remembered now why I only talked to him every couple of months, though we lived in the same town. He was always trying to show how superior he was.

Well, *I* was the bishop, wasn't I? He was only Elders Quorum president in his ward. I had a son serving a mission in Kenya now. Theo's son smoked pot and hardly ever went to church. Theo was never going to end up a god.

"So what's your question?"

"Could the silicon by leaking somehow turn into silicon dioxide?" I asked.

"What an odd question."

"Well, I have this patient who seems to be oozing silicon dioxide from her nipples."

There was silence on the other end of the line.

"Theo?"

"I wonder…"

"What?"

"Victor, I'm just about finished here for the day. Can you stay at your office a little longer? I'd like to take a look at your test results. I assume you've taken an X-ray?"

"Of course."

"Is it okay if I stop by in half an hour?"

"You really think you know what's going on?" It would be irritating if he was the one to figure out the answer, but it was why I'd called, wasn't it? A true Latter-day Saint looked for truth wherever it could be found, even if I had to swallow my pride in front of my know-it-all brother.

"Maybe."

"I have to get home for dinner early so I can get over to the church tonight. You know how it is being bishop."

"Sure. Sure. I'll be over in a few minutes."

I studied the test results again and looked at the X-ray another time, trying to come up with an answer before Theo came. I was still stymied when he arrived, and I explained the case as best I could.

"What do you make of this?" Theo pointed to an area of light streaks on the X-ray.

"It doesn't look normal," I admitted, "but I've seen lots of pictures in textbooks of leakage, and it doesn't look like that, either."

"Does it look intact?"

I paused. "No," I admitted. "I suppose I'd better go in and see if there is leakage. I just don't know."

"Could this be silicon fibrils?" Theo asked, pointing.

"Fibrils? I don't see how. Gel doesn't turn into fibrils, even if it does leak."

"It could if her breasts have come alive."

I stared at Theo. Was he serious? Probably he was trying to pull my leg so he could make fun of me later. It wouldn't be the first time. "Do you use the same drug dealer your son goes to?" I bit my lip, but Theo didn't seem to react.

"All life on Earth is carbon-based," said Theo, "because carbon is tetravalent. It can form four bonds because of its outer electron shell. It usually bonds with other carbons, or oxygen, hydrogen, or nitrogen."

"I know what tetravalent means. I went to medical school, you know."

"So you realize that silicon is also tetravalent. It's right under carbon in the periodic table."

"What has that got to do with my patient's breasts?"

"We've tried thousands of ways to try to create silicon-based life, always without success. But sooner or later, it's possible it will just develop spontaneously on its own, just like carbon-based life had to do at some point."

"And you think the first sign of life will be in a middle-aged woman's tits?"

"Oh, I seriously doubt it. But I always keep my eyes open. I wouldn't mind winning a Nobel prize."

"What about me? She's *my* patient, after all."

"Okay. Okay. I just want you to do some tests that won't hurt her breasts if, well, if they *are* alive."

Theo explained what he wanted me to do, and I called Sister Anderson to ask her to come in Monday before her

Tuesday MRI. She seemed anxious to comply, and on Sunday, she pulled me aside after Sacrament meeting. "Can we meet in the Bishop's office?"

"I have to interview one of the deacons." His mother was concerned about him masturbating, wasting his seed needlessly. Frankly, unless the mother intended to send her son to a fertility clinic every week for the next ten years, the boy wasn't going to be using his seed for anything else much more useful.

"Can you reschedule?"

"Sure."

I took the boy into my office and closed the door. "Your sperm may well have a life force in addition to its fertile properties," I said bluntly. "And bringing it forth a couple of times a week will only make you feel more alive than not doing it will, so I wouldn't worry about it."

It was one of the inconsistencies I found in Mormon attitudes toward sexuality. Only sex within marriage was acceptable. I could accept that extramarital sex was wrong, but what of amarital sex? If you were unmarried, you weren't allowed to be sexual even with yourself. I did hope I was up to the challenge of Celestial sexuality, but I very much wanted to believe I wouldn't be left completely out in the cold if I didn't make it.

And if we only had these few years on Earth to be sexual, I didn't want to deprive this boy of what little time he had. If he wasn't even dating yet, I figured it was safe enough to let him beat off once in a while. Perhaps it was a sin to have non-procreative sex, but lots of older married couples did it all the time, so what was so bad about a young person doing something non-procreative?

At best, we only created six or seven other lives while we were here on Earth. Sally and I had just three children. We had been looked down on for years for our lack of commitment in bringing forth life. Theo had four children, but after my three, I just didn't want any more.

I was afraid this left me a less than Celestial person, so I'd sneaked off to a fertility clinic myself a few times to donate. I always bought Sally a little gift with the money I made. It was right after my twelfth visit that I was called to be a bishop. I couldn't help but feel there was a connection.

I smiled at the boy, and he turned red as I leaned over toward him. "Just don't let your mom catch you anymore." He nodded, and I shooed him out of the office quickly and then ushered Sister Anderson in.

"Bishop, I'm concerned."

"Do you have any new symptoms?"

"Look."

She unbuttoned the front of her dress and let it fall off her shoulders. Then she pulled off her top garment. When I saw Mormon underwear in my physician's office, I didn't think much about it. But seeing them now in my bishop's office, I couldn't help but focus on the little symbols over the nipples, the L to symbolize an arm raised to the square, to remind us to remain righteous always, and the V to remind us of a compass, so that we'd keep ourselves focused on our ultimate goal and destination.

"I don't see anything."

Sister Anderson sighed in frustration. "Bishop, they're *bigger*. They're swollen."

"Do they hurt?"

Sister Anderson shook her head. "They feel fine. In fact, they feel better than ever. There's always a warm, tingly sensation that makes me feel—they feel fine."

I palpated her breasts. They didn't feel quite normal, but I couldn't put my finger on exactly what was different. It reminded me of my first attempts at phlebotomy. I'd palpate someone's arm to feel their veins, and even when I could physically see the vein I was touching, I couldn't feel anything with my fingers at first. It took a great deal of practice before I could detect veins with my fingertips. I had the feeling that if I just knew what I was looking for, I could feel it in Sister Anderson's breasts now.

"Sister Anderson, I have a delicate question." I couldn't call her Valerie in church.

"Yes?"

"Have you and President Anderson ever done anything…strange…to your breasts since the implants?"

Sister Anderson blushed. "Well, naturally Geoff put his hands on them and gave me a blessing with his consecrated oil, that they'd be as lifelike as if they were real."

"Uh huh."

"And, you see, Geoff has this machine with electrodes he puts on his muscles to make them contract. It's his way of exercising while we watch TV. Only PBS, of course."

"Of course."

"So anyway, we put the electrodes on my breasts a couple of times to see if, well, you know."

I really didn't, but I nodded.

"And Geoff's sister is an herbalist, so one day she gave me vitamin injections."

"In your breasts?"

She nodded. "We really wanted my breasts to be as normal as possible. Geoff loves them so."

I shook my head. "But a needle may have punctured them, Sister Anderson. They might very well be leaking."

"Oh, dear."

There was a knock on the door, and I felt a rush of adrenalin. What if I were discovered in my office with a half-naked woman? I'd be released as bishop. I might even be excommunicated. Wouldn't Theo love that?

"Who is it?" I asked through the closed door.

"It's President Anderson. Is Valerie in there?"

I opened the door a crack, and since no one else was in the hall, I quickly let him in and locked the door again. President Anderson walked over to his wife and gave her a peck on the lips. She was still unclothed, and I felt awkward, but I put my hands back on her left breast.

"Let me try one more time to feel what might be going on."

As I palpated Sister Anderson's left breast, President Anderson felt her right one, smiling. I started sensing an erection and hoped it wouldn't show through my suit pants.

"What do you think?"

I shook my head. "Maybe it's a little spongier than gel-like. We'll do more tests tomorrow. If you're feeling well, there's certainly no emergency, whatever may be happening. Everything's going to be okay."

Sister Anderson put her clothes back on, the three of us said a prayer together for the health of her breasts, and then the two of them left. I sighed and let in my next congregant, a computer geek who kept getting in trouble for creating viruses.

Sister Anderson was due in my clinic office at 10:00 the next day, and since my 9:00 canceled when I got in at 8:30, I called Theo to see if he wanted to come by earlier so we could talk. I told him what I'd learned yesterday, letting slip who the patient was, and he laughed.

"You think it's funny she may be leaking?"

"Victor, she's a wonderful experiment."

"She's a person."

"Okay. Okay. But just think about it. Silicon makes up over 25% of the Earth's crust. It's everywhere. And it's not like it isn't already utilized by other life forms. Diatoms use it as a component in their cell walls. Lots of plants, especially grasses, use it in metabolism."

"So you're back to believing her breasts are alive?"

Theo shrugged, still smiling. "Did she have sand on her nipples at church yesterday?"

"Yes."

"The biggest reason silicon doesn't seem to be used in most life forms is because of the difficulty it has in oxidizing. When carbon oxidizes during respiration, it forms carbon dioxide as waste, which is fairly easy to get rid of. But silicon forms silicon dioxide—sand—and a solid is a lot harder to eliminate."

I was confused. "So you think…"

"All that sand coming from her nipples, who knows? I still don't see how even if those implants had come to life, they'd be able to use someone's body structures for their own benefit. Symbiosis is usually an evolved process, not a first-time event. But perhaps this thing is parasitic rather than independent."

I still wondered if Theo was pulling my leg. "Wouldn't something like that be too alien to coexist with us?"

He shook his head. "I don't see why. It's harmless enough. That's why you use silicon in the first place. We already use it in the body in lots of other ways. It's used in artificial joints and heart valves, as a tissue expander, as prostheses for the skeletal system, in ophthalmology, in penile prostheses, like the one you need."

"But life?"

Theo shrugged. "Silicon is used as a facilitator in nerve regeneration. I *guess* it could happen."

He didn't know any more than I did.

I frowned. "Doesn't life grow? Won't it reproduce? Are we going to have baby breast implants running around?"

"We'll have to deal with that when we get to it. Maybe it would have a maximum adult size. Or perhaps we'd need to do a Caesarian on her breasts."

"Maybe we should just try to take the whole thing out right now. I could schedule her for surgery."

"It might not be able to live on its own."

"How do we test for life when all our tests are based on assuming a carbon base?"

"The real question is what we're going to name this new species. I was thinking *Theophilus silicansis.* What do you think?"

"*You* get to name it?"

"You want it to be called *Victorianus something-or-other*?"

"It doesn't have to be *–anus.*"

"Okay. Okay. How about *Senogenitus silicansis*?"

"Hmm." I thought for a moment. "Maybe."

Theo laughed. "You know, Patricia and I have talked about creating silicon-based life on our own planet one day."

Like he'd ever make it to the Celestial Kingdom with that shrew of a wife. I tried not to snort. "Well, *I'm* the one who put those implants in."

"Yes, but it was President and Sister Anderson who brought them to life, and me who discovered it."

"Whatever."

We talked for another fifteen minutes until Sister Anderson arrived. Theo refused to leave the examination room. "Oh, hi, Brother Taylor," Sister Anderson said nervously.

"Do you mind if my brother takes part in the exam?" I asked. "He's a chemist and may be able to offer some insight into what may be going on chemically."

"I suppose that would be all right."

"I'm going to need a biopsy, and in addition to your MRI tomorrow, I've also scheduled you for a CT scan afterward."

"Do you think the cancer is back?"

"No, we think…" I paused. "…some unique biological process may be occurring."

Sister Anderson frowned. "Well, my breasts feel even larger today than they did yesterday. Geoff seems to like that well enough, but all this grit is driving him to distraction."

"Perhaps you should wear a bathing suit and pretend you're on a beach, like in *From Here to Eternity*. Some men find sand sexy."

"My brother has a poor sense of humor," I said. "Sister Anderson, let's get on with the exam. Would you mind disrobing?"

"In front of your brother?"

I nodded and she complied reluctantly. Theo's face was as eager and excited as a schoolboy's. There was a reason the Church didn't approve of members drinking Coke, but Theo felt he was above such rules. Pride was always one of his weaknesses. He could learn a thing or two about humility from me, but he was always so sure he was best.

When it had become clear Theo and I were heading for different career paths, my mother had said, "It's good for the boys to have lives of their own." But I could tell she secretly favored Theo.

As I prepared the biopsy needle, Theo approached Sister Anderson. She eyed him warily.

"I've just got to feel for myself," he said. It wasn't a request for permission. He reached over and gently squeezed Sister Anderson's right breast.

"Bishop Taylor—"

"It twitched! I felt it twitch!"

"Theo, get a hold of yourself."

"*Senogenitus silicansis*. I'll be famous."

"*We'll* be famous."

"Bishop Taylor?"

"*I* discovered this. You don't know enough freshman chemistry to make any connections. *I* get the credit because I deserve it."

"Like hell." I pulled Theo away from Sister Anderson.

"I'll bet there's even chirality. Look, her right breast is probably the mirror image of the left. What a breakthrough that would be if it was happening at the molecular level."

"I want you to leave now, Theo."

"I won't. I'm taking part in every test from now on. *I'll* make the determination. You were always the leech. You'd never have made it through med school without me. I wrote half your papers."

"Theo, you promised never—"

"Bishop Taylor?"

I walked to a drawer and opened it, pulling out a scalpel. I showed it to Theo. He laughed.

"You need to leave," I said. "This is my patient, my implant, my discovery. I'm taking the credit. We'll see who becomes famous."

"What are you two fighting about?"

"Your breasts are alive. It's a new species. A new order of life altogether. Nothing like it has ever existed on this planet before."

"Shut up, Theo. I'll handle this."

"I knew it! I felt something the instant Geoff gave me a blessing."

"Well, *he's* not taking credit!" I said quickly. "Hey!" I hadn't noticed, but Theo had moved toward a drawer, and now he had a scalpel, too.

"Take the biopsy," said Theo. "Let's get these tests done. One for your lab, and one for mine."

"I thought I was going to be an android or something, but this is even better."

"Get out, Theo."

"I'll do the biopsy myself."

"Bishop Taylor, I don't want any more tests."

I lunged at Theo and slashed down at his arm, drawing blood in a long line. I felt a tingling in my groin. Theo shouted and lunged back, cutting a slice across my chest. He cut my nipple. For some reason, this seemed more insulting than just cutting regular skin. I was so mad I thrust again, stabbing Theo in the stomach. Blood spurted from the wound. Theo waved his scalpel and ripped half my ear off.

It smarted.

Sister Anderson stood off to the side squealing while I tried everything I could to kill Theo. He was Jacob, plotting to steal my birthright. Sister Anderson would testify for me in a Church court, and I wouldn't be excommunicated. She'd testify for me in a secular court, too. *I* was her doctor. *I'd* saved her breasts. *I'd* saved her marriage because of the implants.

That bastard Theo was trying to ruin everything, just like he'd done when he told my first fiancée' I wasn't a virgin and then dated her himself. Here I'd actually created life and he just wanted to confiscate it for himself. I never did trust PhD's.

And Mom and Dad had bought *him* a house when he graduated, when all they got me was a car.

I lunged again and sank the scalpel into Theo's neck. He kicked me and stabbed into my chest. He slipped on some blood and fell to the floor, but he didn't get up. I leaned over him, panting heavily. "I—brought—forth—life," I wheezed.

Then I fell next to Theo on the floor. My hand was resting on his chest, and he picked it up with disgust and thrust it away.

I lay on the floor, my blood mixing with Theo's. I hoped Sister Anderson would go alert my secretary and get me help. I looked up at her. She was staring down at her breasts, petting them softly. "Sister Anderson," I managed to say but could get no further.

"Come on, my babies," she said, pulling her clothes up over her breasts, "let's go home and talk to Daddy."

I watched weakly as Sister Anderson picked up her purse. She walked over and stood above me. "You know, Bishop," she said slowly, "it's not really like having a baby. That's more like…like a prolongation of your own life. This is creating entirely new life. I bet Geoff and I get translated soon. We won't even have to wait for the resurrection. We're practically gods now."

She started to turn away and then looked back. "I'll have Geoff come to the hospital and give you guys a blessing. Maybe some part of you will come to life, too."

"Maybe his brain," whispered Theo.

"Maybe his heart," I panted back.

"Maybe his balls," Theo grunted.

I realized then that my penis had been hard throughout the entire fight. It was starting to wilt now, and I worried again about my chances of enjoying eternal erections. Surely, the act of creating life would outweigh my attempt to eradicate it, especially since I was so completely justified.

Life simply had to trump death. That must be why I could get a hard-on even while attacking my brother. The life force had to show its superiority.

I began to feel very sleepy. I looked over at Theo, who was already asleep. Sister Anderson was walking out of the office, and I looked up at the light in the ceiling, thinking of God.

Perhaps after I recovered, I could go to another plastic surgeon and get a silicon prosthetic enlargement for my penis, and maybe I could get it to come to life, too, follow whatever protocol the Andersons had used. And even though Sally's breasts were perfectly healthy, I could put some implants in her as well.

I was going to be a god. I was going to be famous. *Victorianus* my ass. *Senogenitus* might be okay for the breasts, but I'd call my living penis *Victoropenosis silicansis*.

Something victorious.

This was just the beginning. I might even be promoted in the Church to apostle, and who knows, perhaps even prophet one day. I was a great man, as I always knew I would be. Who was Theo to judge? He didn't even pay a full tithe. And he had bad breath, too.

I heard a scream and looked up to see my secretary, Ann, staring down at me in horror. But I felt okay. Just a little tired. Being a god was hard work. I smiled up at Ann. Then I closed my eyes, more relaxed than I'd felt in ages, and let myself dream of the awards I was bound to win.

The Ghost of Emma Smith

I was fourteen when I had my first vision. I was walking upstairs to my bedroom with a headache, intending to lie down for a half hour, but when I entered my room, there was a woman sitting on my bed wearing old-fashioned clothing. My mouth fell open, but I remembered my manners.

"Hello," I said. I actually curtseyed, having watched a movie the day before where a lady did this when meeting important people.

The woman on the bed smiled, raised herself up, and faded away.

I stood there in astonishment for several moments. I was terribly sleepy, but I knew I hadn't imagined this. I felt alert enough now to go to my parents' bedroom. My mother was taking a nap.

I shook her shoulder, and after several moments, she looked up groggily. "What is it, Eliza?"

"I think I just saw Emma Smith."

My mother sighed, and I explained what had happened. At that point, she sat up in her bed, looking worried. "Ever since we moved here in November, I've had the feeling we weren't alone. I wonder why the ghost appeared to you?" She looked at me sharply. "It certainly wasn't Emma Smith. This house isn't old enough. It was just some other woman who lived here before us. Do you suppose she's never moved on? Can a person sneak out of the Spirit World? Only resurrected people can really act as messengers, not spirits."

My family had always lived in Palmyra, and we loved staying where the Mormon Church was founded. Being Mormon in Palmyra influenced everything we did. We'd lived in a 1960's-era house most of my life, then one built in the 1950's, and two months ago, we'd moved into this old home built in the 1920's. It was a move up for us, a stately old house, even if in a bit of disrepair.

The furnace clanked heavily, but the plumbing seemed sound, though Dad had said we'd need to replace the hot water heater soon. We eventually wanted to find a house that had actually been around back in 1830, but those were hard to find and very expensive. My mother was the driving force behind our going backward to older and older houses. My father would sigh whenever my mother found a new prospect, but he liked antiques and seemed to want the simpler way of life an old house represented, so he went along with the moves.

"I know why she appeared to me," I said timidly.

"Now, I won't have any more of that, Eliza."

I nodded and went back to my room. I knew, though, that it was time for a new direction in the Church. I'd read the Book of Mormon and the Doctrine and Covenants and parts of the Bible. Women might be the mothers of nations, the mothers of prophets, of the Messiah himself, but they were still afterthoughts.

I realized, however, that it was time for a woman to become a prophet. I was fourteen now, the same age Joseph Smith had been, and in the same town he'd lived in, when he had his first vision. I knew it was my destiny.

The fact that it was Emma Smith who had appeared to me, and not Adam or Moroni or Peter, told me I was right.

I knelt beside my bed and prayed. "Heavenly Father, I'm ready. Please send Emma back to me."

I stayed on my knees half an hour and eventually grew tired and fell asleep on the floor beside my bed.

Over the next several days, I continued to feel the presence of an unseen being. I began talking to her when I was alone, in case she could hear me. It seemed to happen most often in the late evening or early morning. At school, there was no hint of prophetic inspiration. I couldn't even pass my algebra tests. And in the afternoon when I came home, I felt completely alone in my room. It was only as the evening dragged on into the late hours that I could feel Emma trying to reach me again.

One Saturday, when I was in the kitchen with Mom, my little brother Samuel came up to us. "What do you want, Mom?"

She looked at him and laughed. "What do you mean?"

"I heard you calling and calling."

Mom looked at me and then back at Samuel. "No one's been calling you, dear."

"Sure you were."

"I've been here all along," I offered. "Mom never called."

Samuel stomped his foot. "Real funny," he said and stormed off.

Mom looked at me quizzically, but I looked away, irritated. Had Emma Smith been calling to Samuel? Was I being passed over for yet another male? Had I done something wrong? Not displayed enough faith? Samuel was only eleven. It seemed very unfair for him to get to be a prophet.

My headaches seemed worse over the weekend, though I usually felt better after getting out of the house for a few hours on Sunday for church. I began hearing bells ringing in the middle of the night, and once I woke up with the vivid sensation that someone was strangling me. I fought off the attacker and turned on my lamp, only to find the room empty.

I felt a chill run through me. I remembered that just before Joseph Smith's first vision, he was attacked by unseen hands, too. I was happy to know I was still being considered for the position of prophetess, if unnerved as well.

One evening during dinner, when the whole family was around the kitchen table, there wasn't much talking, unusual for us. Everybody seemed to be in a bad mood or depressed or feeling nauseated. I had lost my appetite but was forcing myself to eat because I knew my mother always worked hard on dinner.

"The green beans came out really good," I said.

Mom nodded listlessly.

I looked at my brother. "Sam, what did you study in English today?"

"We read a story about ghosts," he said glumly. "I told my teacher we had ghosts in our house, and she gave me punishwork to do."

"Well, we certainly don't have ghosts," my dad said firmly. "Don't be ridiculous."

"Doesn't the Church teach that our spirits go on after we die?" I asked. "Why can't there be ghosts?"

"Spirits go to the Spirit World or Spirit Prison after they die," said my mother. "They don't hang around here."

"But you said—"

My mother shook her head at me sharply.

"I saw a woman in my room," said Samuel.

"You most certainly did not," my father replied.

"Joseph Smith saw ghosts," I offered.

Mother put her fork down and looked at my father nervously. "He did not. He saw resurrected beings. There's a big difference." I looked at my father, who was rolling his eyes. It irritated me.

"But they were still dead people," I insisted. "I think Emma Smith has been coming here. *I* saw her once, too." I looked at my brother for confirmation. He was staring at his plate queasily.

"I won't tolerate another word on the subject," my father said. "I—"

"Do you hear that?" I interrupted, holding out my hand over the table to shush everyone.

"What?"

"Footsteps upstairs!"

Everyone listened. "I don't hear a thing."

"It's as plain as your snoring at night. And it's coming from my room!" I jumped up from the table and hurtled up the stairs two at a time. I threw open the door to my room and looked about.

My father and mother were right behind me. "Well?" my father demanded.

"I don't see her," I said in disappointment. "But I'm sure that—"

"Oh, good grief. The Church has poisoned you with all this nonsense. There are no prophets, no visions, not even any Spirit World. It's all superstition."

"Oh, Mark, how can you say such a thing?"

"Dad, you're going to get us zapped. We'll all die in our sleep."

"Anybody up here?" asked Samuel.

"No. We're going back downstairs to finish our dinner."

"I'm not hungry."

"Get back downstairs."

Maybe my dad was the reason Emma was hesitant in appearing to me. Joseph Smith had supportive parents, and even a prophet needs support if he's only fourteen. I had to convince Emma to come see me even if my father was an apostate.

I left little notes for Emma in my room the next day, and I fasted on Friday. Saturday morning, I read more of a biography on Emma, and Saturday afternoon while I was praying for God to call upon me, I fell asleep beside my bed.

I woke up later with a splitting headache, and my vision was a little blurry. But I could distinctly feel someone else in the room with me.

"Emma?" I asked.

I heard rustling and stood up to look around. Right in front of my dresser was a woman. I couldn't tell if it was the same person I'd seen before, but I started walking toward her, smiling. She began walking toward me as well.

"What can you tell me?" I asked. "What's the revelation? My news for the world?"

There was no response, and I stopped walking. Emma did, too. Then as my vision cleared, I saw that I was looking at my reflection in the mirror. Had it all been a mistake?

I shook my head. I was *sure* there had been someone else in the room. Perhaps when I stopped walking toward her, I demonstrated a lack of faith and made her disappear. Why hadn't I gone up to embrace her?

Sunday, Dad said he felt too sick to go to church, but we all suspected that after his confession of faithlessness, he was just trying to avoid taking the sacrament. I couldn't do a complete fast again so soon, but I skipped breakfast, asking for God to touch my father's heart and to send Emma back.

Maybe Emma could tell me how I could reach into my father's soul. Saving my own family would be as important as anything I could do for the Church.

I confided in my friend Shelly after Sunday School what had been happening. I tried not to be obnoxious about my privileged status, but I still expected her to be impressed.

She was not.

"Oh, Eliza! That house is haunted. I meant to tell you when you moved in, but I didn't want to scare you. The family that lived there before all reported seeing and hearing strange things, and then one day they were all found dead in their beds. You've got to get out of there."

I was dumbfounded. Could Shelly be right? We were told that Satan could appear as an angel of light. Were these spirits in our house evil rather than good? Was I really not about to be chosen as a prophet? Maybe the woman in my room was the wife of one of the early persecutors.

Still, I thought, if I was in tune enough with the Spirit World to see this much, I could ask for more. I could still see Emma if my heart was pure.

I went to my dad's bedside after I returned home and put my hand on his head. He smiled weakly. "Hi, honey."

"Still feeling rotten?"

"I have a terrible headache."

I hesitated a moment and then blurted out, "I know I don't have the priesthood, but I can still give you a blessing."

Dad frowned.

"I've seen Emma Smith twice now. I can ask her to see that you're healed. On the other side, I bet women *do* hold the priesthood. I think—"

Dad forced himself to sit up. "Eliza, I'm going to have to forbid you to ever go back to church."

"What?"

"I thought it would be harmless to let kids have some socializing outside of school. But I can see these toxic teachings just go on seeping insidiously into your brain."

"Dad, it's all true. Emma—"

"I'm taking away your Church books. From now on, you'll read classics, or science books, or history books."

"My biography of Emma is a history book."

"That does it."

Dad swung his legs to the floor and stood up in his underwear. He wore just boxers and a T-shirt, not the special garments Mom wore after they went through the temple. It made me sad to see him so decadent.

Dad headed toward my room, and I suddenly realized what he was up to. "No, Dad!" I said. "You can't. The Church is good. The Church is true. I'm going to be a prophet. I—"

Dad pushed open my door and walked into the room, with me only a step behind. He stopped abruptly and stared at my dresser. I frowned.

"Oh my god."

"What?"

"There's a woman in your room."

Now my *dad* was having a vision? My heart started beating faster. *He* wasn't going to steal my revelations away, was he? I remembered that Paul and Alma the Younger and the sons of Mosiah had all been wicked and then seen miraculous visions and become great men.

It wasn't *fair*. I was the one who was always good. I was the one the Church needed. Why were men always chosen over women? I stomped my foot.

"Emma!" I called. "I want you to appear to me right now!"

My father collapsed on the floor, and I reached down to revive him. There was no response. It was just like King Lamoni. I ran to get my mother. She called an ambulance, and soon we were all at the hospital awaiting word. Had my father been struck down like Korihor for doubting? Were we going to lose him? Perhaps his illness was just to provide a way for me to show the power of women when I healed him later.

After a long while, the doctor came over to us, smiling grimly. "It looks like your husband is suffering carbon monoxide poisoning. I expect you all are. You'll have to leave your home until you can get it checked out and repair whatever gas appliances are causing the problem."

My mouth fell open.

"Have you been experiencing headaches?" the doctor went on. "Hearing noises? Seeing things?"

I closed my mouth and could feel my jaw clench. This man was *not* going to take away my visions. It was a lie, a tool of the devil to shake my faith. If I proved myself strong now, I could still earn my place among the prophets.

"Do you have somewhere to stay?" the doctor asked.

"Yes" My mother rubbed her forehead. "We're friendly with the neighbors next door."

"Good. But first, let's see if we need to admit any of the rest of you to the hospital."

We submitted to the blood tests, and before long, we heard the verdict. My mother would have to stay in the hospital at least overnight while receiving pure oxygen. Samuel and I had to breathe it for a couple of hours, but we were allowed to go to the neighbors' house as long as we came back for another dose of oxygen tomorrow.

Mom called Mrs. Thompson, who agreed to come pick us up. Samuel and I ate dinner with them, and then we were ushered off to bed, Sam sharing her son Allen's room, since Allen was in Sam's class at school, and me getting the guest room all to myself.

Lying in bed in the dark, I thought about what to do. Even if it were true that my visions were caused by carbon monoxide, I had to wonder if that wasn't a viable catalyst for enlightenment, like peyote or LSD or any of the other things people used. Emma hadn't been a hallucination. I had truly seen her. And I wanted to see her again.

After the Thompsons were finally asleep, I put on my shoes and slipped out the back door. It was especially cold tonight, and I wanted to make sure to get enough gas to compensate for several hours out of the house, so I turned up the furnace. It was like seeding a cloud, I decided. Joan of Arc might have been schizophrenic to receive her visions, but she was still a prophet, even if not recognized by the Church.

For all I knew, Joseph Smith had been bipolar or schizophrenic himself. But that didn't keep him from being one of the greatest prophets of all time. So maybe I simply needed carbon monoxide to put me in tune with God.

But I *was* going to do it. I was going to be a prophet.

I opened the vent in my bedroom more fully, knelt beside my bed, and started praying.

I prayed longer and harder than I'd ever prayed before. I swore eternal chastity, vowed to raise eight children, promised to serve eighteen months as a missionary, said I'd finally finish reading the Bible. I explained why I felt it was so important to finally get a woman's perspective in the Church, though I insisted I would follow whatever advice was revealed to me. I committed myself to ensuring the continual growth of the gospel and the obedience of the saints.

"Nothing is more important to me than being useful to the Church," I prayed aloud. "I can make a difference. I can. Please use me."

After three hours on my knees, though, I discovered Satan trying to sneak his way into my mind. Letting myself be poisoned was reckless, my neurons told me. If I could only lead the righteous through brain damage, perhaps there was something wrong with the righteous as well. Maybe no one throughout history had ever seen God. Perhaps every vision ever recorded was a simple matter of brain chemistry.

I decided to get up and go back next door. But it was late and I was so very tired. I stretched out my legs and leaned against the side of the bed. Just a quick nap and I'd go downstairs and leave the house.

I'd study Joseph Smith's visions and those of others more carefully. Maybe it was all still true. And if it was, I'd manage to find a way to join their ranks. But it was too late to worry about that now. I needed to rest my heavy eyelids for just a moment.

I closed my eyes. The house felt so warm and comfortable.

"Eliza."

"Eliza."

I opened my eyes. Emma Smith was standing before me.

"You must leave this house immediately. There are important things in your future."

"Really?"

"Get up and go."

I stood beside the bed, holding onto it for a moment to catch my balance. When I looked up, Emma was gone.

But she'd spoken to me this time, which she hadn't done before.

I walked down the stairs and back to the Thompsons' house. I fell asleep almost immediately, and I had a terrible headache when I awoke in the morning.

We had our furnace repaired, and the headaches and queasiness and footsteps and voices and visions stopped. I never saw Emma Smith again, and I never knew if that last vision of her was real or not. I gave a long talk on Emma in church one day, and a report on carbon monoxide in science class, and eventually I graduated both from high school and Seminary.

I did go on to serve a mission, marry in the temple, and have two children of my own.

But I never did have another revelation. My father eventually stopped going to church and even had his name removed from the records. Samuel also stopped his church attendance, never even going on a mission as I had. Mom died last year, still active in the Church.

I miss those early days in our last house, the joy and wonderment mixed with the headaches and nausea. But I have carbon monoxide detectors in my own home now, and neither of my two daughters has ever seen a vision.

I'm not sure if I'm doing them a favor or not. I hope one of them will be a prophet one day, but only if their visions are real.

If such things actually exist to begin with.

I have a painting of Emma Smith on my bedroom wall. I look at it often and hope.

Food for Lack of Thought

I took the metal scoop and filled it with a cup's worth of dried popcorn kernels. My companion, Sister Ross, was holding a plastic bag open, and I poured the kernels into it. Sister Ross then tied the bag like a balloon while I scooped another cup of dried kernels.

"Isn't this fun, Sister Clayton?" My companion grinned at me like a little child playing dress up in her mother's clothes.

"Sure."

I poured another scoop of kernels into the next bag, and Sister Ross nudged me. "Come on," she said with a smile. "What does this make you think of?" She waited a second while I looked at her blankly. "Come on. Come on, you know."

I scooped up another cup of dried kernels, and my companion began singing. "I looked out the window and what did I see?" She paused, grinning like a hyena. "Come on, Sister Clayton, come on? What did you see?"

"Popcorn," I said. I poured my scoop into Sister Ross's waiting bag.

"That's right!" she gushed. "Isn't this fun?" She tied the plastic bag.

We were working in Georgetown at Lifelong AIDS Alliance, preparing food to be delivered to various patients. The organization had started out focusing on people with AIDS, but those folks were living so long these days that the group had expanded their focus to any other patients who also suffered from debilitating diseases. Sister Ross and I volunteered in the warehouse four hours a week for our community service.

Some weeks, if I was tired of missionary work, we volunteered a second day for another four hours, in the kitchen cooking for the Chicken Soup Brigade. We usually did that on Sunday, the absolute last day of the week I wanted to be proselytizing. I'd just announced to my companion we'd be coming back this Sunday as well.

But Sister Ross stomped her foot and shook her bag of popcorn kernels at me. "It's wrong to work on the Sabbath," she said.

"We're not working," I told her again. "We're volunteering."

"Still," she said. "My mother always cooked the simplest meal of the week on Sunday, to avoid working hard. If we can't do it for ourselves, we shouldn't do it for others, either."

"My mother always made the biggest meal of the week on Sunday," I countered. "It was like a holiday every week." I looked at her. "You do know that's where the word comes from. Holy Day. You're supposed to have big meals on holidays."

"Like Yom Kippur?" my companion asked. Her lip curled in a slight sneer. How she could go from chipper to bitter in thirty seconds always amazed me. My mood was always pretty constant.

I shrugged. "We sometimes bought fried chicken on the way home from church."

"And made other poor girls work on the Sabbath," Sister Ross concluded.

I shrugged again. "They weren't Mormon," I said. "They didn't have the same commandments we did."

"*Everyone* is supposed to obey *all* the commandments *all* the time."

"Okay, okay," I conceded. "We can either work here four hours on Sunday or six hours on Monday. Which do you prefer?" I was honestly perfectly okay with either option. I could spend half a day here every day and be fine with it.

"I choose Monday," she said.

"Monday it is. Thanks for keeping me on the strait and narrow."

Sister Ross frowned, apparently unsure if she'd won the argument or not. It was a technique I used with her often. We continued filling bags with popcorn kernels until we emptied the bin in front of us. Our next task was to set up paper grocery bags along both sides of an aisle, two bags deep, and put one plastic bag of popcorn kernels in each. Then we were to put one can of yams in each bag. And then make yet another round putting one box of tea in each bag. The items were different each time we volunteered, just whatever Lifelong had on hand at the time.

"I don't feel comfortable giving people tea," said Sister Ross.

"Let's sing 'Popcorn Popping on the Apricot Tree' again," I suggested. My companion's eyes lit up, and she started belting out the Primary children's song. I knew she was hoping we could use it as a missionary tool, that one of the other workers would ask us about it, leading to an appointment, a lesson, and then a baptism.

Like that ever happened.

After three rounds of stooping down over the paper bags, my back started to hurt. We'd been asked to add several more items to the bags, but I thought we should try a different task first to give us a break. "Ready for more scooping?" I asked. "We're supposed to divide this bin of rice into plastic bags, like we did for the popcorn."

"Sure!" Sister Ross enthused. "Scooping is fun!" She grabbed a plastic bag and held it out in front of me, waiting. Soon we were in the middle of another monotonous routine. That was perhaps what I liked best about volunteering here—I could forget about everything and empty my mind.

Only I could never really empty my mind. That was part of the problem. I thought about Sister Turnley who we were trying to reactivate. She was a lesbian, between girlfriends, and debating whether or not celibacy was worse than heartbreak. I held her while she cried each time we left her apartment.

Then there was Sister Piper, an elderly widow who had difficulty coming to church, so she was officially deemed "inactive," even though her testimony was as strong as anyone's. But the elders couldn't come over to give her the sacrament because she was a single woman. And we couldn't give her the sacrament because we didn't hold the priesthood. And no one ever seemed able to arrange for both men and women to visit her at the same time, so that it would be safe for everyone.

"Are you happy?" I asked, pouring a scoop of dry rice into a plastic bag.

"Of course," Sister Ross replied. "Aren't you?"

I dug my metal scoop deep into the rice bin. "My brother has left the Church."

"Oh, no! How terrible!" She reached over and touched my elbow.

My brother had just finished his film degree at Loyola Marymount in Los Angeles and found his first menial job in the profession. If he worked his way up, it would be difficult for him not to be influenced by all those liberals out in Hollywood. Unless, of course, he became a Scientologist instead. I knew I should feel bad for him, but Cary having a new cultural norm wasn't much different from me starting to root for the Seahawks now that I was living in Seattle.

Or for me to start identifying with all the atheists here in the Pacific Northwest. If there were atheists in St. George, they were pretty closeted.

"How would you feel if one of your kids didn't make it to the Celestial Kingdom with you?" I asked.

"It would be just awful." She paused. "Just awful." Sister Ross stared at her full bag of rice, unmoving, until I nudged her to tie it off.

"Could you be happy in the Celestial Kingdom without one of your kids?" I went on. "Be a happy goddess for eternity, knowing one of your children didn't make it?"

"Well, we still get to visit them down in the lower kingdoms, don't we?"

"Like that time we visited Sister Marks in jail after she beat her husband?" The Beehive instructor had discovered her husband was cheating on her and hit him over the head with a ceramic vase.

"I suppose."

I scooped up another cup of rice. And then another. And yet another. Before too much longer, we'd emptied the bin. I wasn't ready to go back to the paper bags on the floor yet. My back was still a little sore from earlier. So I pointed to the bin of dried kidney beans next to the empty rice bin and waved my scoop at Sister Ross. She rubbed her upper arm and nodded.

I thought of Sister Turnley. The last time we'd visited, she'd asked for a blessing. "I know you don't really hold the priesthood," she said, "but I need to feel the touch of another woman, and this seemed the safest way to do that." Sister Ross refused to participate, so I put my hands on Sister Turnley's head by myself.

What did the afterlife hold in store for someone like that?

Or for someone like Sister Ross, who couldn't bring herself to comfort a suffering woman?

Or for me, who wasn't any more effective than my companion?

"My mom says she won't mind Cary not making it to the Celestial Kingdom," I said.

"Why not?" Sister Ross asked. "Doesn't she love him?"

I shrugged. "She says we're supposed to be happy in heaven, and she won't be happy if she knows he's in the Telestial Kingdom. And for that matter, *he* won't be happy if he can't come visit Mom in the Celestial Kingdom."

"So…?"

"So she thinks Heavenly Father will make them forget each other. It's the only way either of them can be happy."

Sister Ross paused while tying a plastic bag. I gave her a moment and then nudged her.

"So…so…?" My companion struggled with the concept.

I couldn't blame her. I had trouble with it as well. I'd asked my mother point blank, "God gives us Celestial roofies to make us forget?"

"Yes," she insisted, "just like the one he gave Mary when he impregnated her with Jesus."

I wasn't sure I could accept that. I desperately wanted to be happy at some point, so I was doing everything I could to make it to the Celestial Kingdom. I accepted there was no happiness in this life, and if I was going to be unhappy anyway, why not do all the miserable things one needed to do to earn the Celestial Kingdom? At least once there I could finally be happy.

I scooped another cup of beans and poured it into Sister Ross's waiting bag.

"How can Heavenly Father be happy?" I asked.

"What do you mean?" My companion tied another bag.

"Heavenly Father has to be aware that one third of his children are in Outer Darkness. No one made *him* forget. How can he ever be happy knowing that so many of his children are in hell forever?"

Sister Ross stared at the plastic bag in her hand.

"For that matter, how can he be happy aside from that, knowing that his *good* children who aren't in hell are suffering through war and famine and terrorism? How can God be happy knowing that bosses are making their employees miserable? That people are being mugged and raped? That they're suffering from cancer and MS and dementia?" I held up my scoop like a sword. "How can God be happy at all?"

"Because…because it's all for our own good," Sister Ross managed.

I stared at the bin full of beans and then closed my eyes for a long moment. I opened them again and dug my scoop down into them, pouring more into another plastic bag. "What if…?" I began. "What if we're *never* going to be happy?" I felt my lip quivering.

Sister Ross made a little sound like a mouse being stepped on. Then she took a deep breath, cleared her throat, and began singing. "I looked out the window and what did I see?"

She continued to sing, one Primary song after another, while we finished emptying the bin of beans. She was silent as we put the beans and rice in all the plastic bags, and she was quick to point out that we'd been at Lifelong for three hours and fifty minutes now, and that was close enough to four hours.

"I'm hungry and I want to go home for lunch." She stomped her foot, and I nodded in agreement.

After we ate, Sister Ross took a nap, but I was too antsy to rest. I looked through our kitchen cabinets, which were all but bare, and found a box of Devil's food cake mix. Sister Ross and I had been saving it to celebrate our first baptism. Then we'd amended that to celebrate our first real investigator.

Then we'd forgotten about it.

I took down the cake mix and pulled out our one mixing bowl, and I started preparing a special treat to bring over to Sister Turnley later this evening.

By Any Means Necessary

"Ugh," I said, "time to fill out our stat sheet again."

"I *hate* having to write Zero for the number of baptisms every week," my companion said. I'd been with Sister Adams for just a few weeks, ever since my emergency transfer here due to an unpleasant situation with her previous comp.

"If we could change 'baptisms' to 'converts,' at least we could write in our own names one week out of the eighteen months we're here."

Sister Adams laughed. "Don't think someone hasn't tried that already," she said.

"We need to go to the temple next Preparation Day so we can count the people we do endowments for," I replied.

Sister Adams shook her head. "That's verboten, too."

"Sheesh," I said. "What in the world do they expect?"

"They expect us to baptize people."

"You show me a General Authority who makes miracles happen daily before you ask *me* to make one as often as they keep asking." Our leaders expected us to go door to door, to hand out pamphlets at bus stops, to sing on street corners, whatever it took to get someone interested.

My singing had yet to stir someone's soul.

Sister Adams laughed. "I had a baptism once, back when I'd been out about three months. I don't remember it very well, but I do have pictures. I can look them up sometime and show you."

"No, no, I believe you," I said. "I believe there are people who win the lottery, too. And people who become big movie stars. And people who win Nobel prizes. It just hasn't been my personal experience."

We filled out our stat sheet and sent it to our district leader, along with our letters to the mission president. President Kincaid and his family lived over in Bellevue, so we didn't see them very often. I wondered what it would be like to attend church with him every week.

For that matter, what had it been like to attend services during Jesus's day? There would be Jesus on the stand, smiling pleasantly as some nervous teen gave a youth talk. Trying not to nod off when the ward's notorious old coot rambled on in testimony meeting. Pulling on his beard to make himself stay awake.

It was just as well my companion and I were stationed in the Mt. Baker neighborhood of south Seattle. A little distance from the MP was probably a good thing. Sister Adams and I wrote some Get Well cards for a few of the members we knew were ill.

That included mental illness, as we had one bipolar sister who'd spent a night in jail after a manic episode. It seemed a little odd to wish her "well," when we knew she'd have this illness the rest of her life.

That evening, we visited Sister Garcia, a single mother with two young children. She'd joined the Church by herself a year ago, without a husband, and the bishop didn't want to help her with Church welfare because she didn't pay a full tithe. "I no can afford," she told us. "Why he not help?"

"The Lord will bless you" was all I could manage to say.

On Sunday, instead of attending Relief Society, we walked down to the room where the Laurels were taught. Sister Thompson, the Laurel teacher, had asked us to help her with a special activity for the girls. The Laurels had been all atwitter last week when the Church removed from the Young Women's manual a verse from Moroni which stated that if a girl was raped, she lost her chastity and purity.

It looked like the Church was eventually going to come out of the Dark Ages in its treatment of women, and it was good to see it happening. As soon as we entered the room, Sister Thompson split us up. "Sister Walker, you help Tara," she said. "And Sister Adams, you help Marcy." There were a few other adult women standing next to the other girls.

"Help them with what?" I asked.

"With make-up, of course."

It finally dawned on me that the activity was to prepare the girls for their temple weddings. I helped Tara with her eye shadow and lipstick, making sure none of the make-up touched the bridal gowns that had been loaned by some of the women in the ward. The gowns were all white, naturally, long-sleeved, draping to the floor. Some of them had lace, but only over solid fabric. There were little veils to put over the girls' faces, but they'd be positioned today to stay up out of the way for the photographs.

"Tara," I said, "let's do something special with your hair."

"There's not much I can do," she said with a frown. The girl's hair was mousy brown, thin, and straight, but I managed to eke out two French braids, and Tara's face shone with glee at the transformation.

It didn't take much to make some people happy, I thought. But then, I supposed braids were easier miracles than baptisms. Or getting Church welfare.

After all the girls in class were dressed and fixed up as pretty as they could manage, Sister Thompson pulled out a life-sized cardboard cut-out of a man in a suit, looking every bit like a missionary without the nametag. She set up the figure in front of a large backdrop depicting the Salt Lake temple.

Members were supposed to marry in their local temples, but Bellevue, as lovely as it was, was still no match for Salt Lake.

After all the girls had their pictures taken, we helped everyone de-beautify. The girls left at the end of class to join their families, and Sister Thompson came over to thank us for our help. "It's especially nice when they see sister missionaries," she said, "because that makes the male RMs seem that much more real."

"Oh, they're real, all right," I said, thinking of Elder Rasmussen's smelly farts and Elder Gerard's pimply neck. He really needed to get a better razor.

"And shows them what will happen if they don't catch a man in time," Sister Thompson continued.

I looked at her.

"We used to do this same activity in Young Women when I was a girl, too." Sister Adams studied the photo of the RM. "I did it as a Beehive, and as a MIA Maid, and as a Laurel." She sighed. "Such a sweet activity."

"Have you ever had the girls put on graduation robes and stand in front of a photo of the University of Washington holding a diploma?" I asked.

Both women stared at me in confusion.

A few more days went by with no lessons, no Books of Mormon handed out, no investigators committed to coming to church. In fact, we had no investigators at all. The one man who expressed mild interest we were forced to hand over to the elders to protect our reputations.

And that of the Church. I couldn't face turning in another disappointing stat sheet, but I didn't want to bother the mission president, who had so much on his own plate all the time, so I made an appointment to see the stake president to discuss my woes. I felt I needed someone higher up than just the local bishop, who owned a butcher shop.

"Should we really spend the whole evening at the stake center," my companion asked, "when we should be out finding Golden Contacts? We already spend two hours a week there just so you can practice the piano."

"I think we'd have more success sitting at an intersection with a sign written on a piece of cardboard. 'Will baptize for cookies.'" Of course, that made it sound like we wanted both the baptisms *and* the cookies.

And why shouldn't we, I thought? We were always serving others. It was high time someone served us for a change.

I thought of a Young Women's activity I'd participated in as a teen. Our stake president was hosting a party for some business friends, and all the girls got the opportunity to wait on them. It allowed us the chance to see the kind of men we needed to prepare ourselves for, plus it showed the non-members present what good girls the Mormons were.

"Sister Walker." President Blake shook my hand as I entered his office. "What can I do for you?" He sat down behind his desk and I sat down in front of it. "I must say, it's unusual for one of you young sister missionaries to come and see me." He gave me a grin and a piercing look, both of which lasted just a tad too long.

"I'm unhappy with the number of people I'm bringing to Christ," I said. "I thought the work would move ahead in a much more solid manner than it has."

"And what is it I can do to help you?" he asked.

"I don't know," I admitted. "I guess I just wanted to vent to someone."

He laughed. "Oh, we all know about letting off steam." He continued chuckling. "My two counselors and I have to do it all the time. We carry such a heavy burden for the Church here." He shook his head. "Sometimes, we feel we'll just *explode* if we don't do something drastic." He adjusted his tie.

"And what is it you do to release the pressure?" I asked. Maybe the same thing would work for missionaries. This was exactly the kind of counsel I'd come for.

President Blake looked at me for a long moment without replying. Then he stood up and moved to the front of his desk, sitting on the edge. "Sister," he said, "you remember in the temple when you promised to consecrate everything you owned to further the work of the Lord?"

"Yes?"

"The most basic thing you own is yourself, isn't it?"

I frowned. "I'm not sure I follow."

"Sister," the president said, standing up and walking over to the wall, where he straightened a framed photo of the First Presidency, "do you find it difficult to make ends meet with the money you have available for your missionary work?"

"Of course," I said. "We all do."

"Could you use an extra hundred dollars a week?"

He couldn't possibly be implying what it sounded like he was implying. Could he? Even if he were, I began to wonder if it would really be that big a deal. If the Church were true, and I believed it was, then I was probably only going to make it to the Telestial Kingdom in any event. It was like being "a little bit pregnant." Once I was damned, the exact degree hardly mattered.

How could a missionary who hadn't brought a single soul to the gospel in her entire mission make it any higher than the Telestial Kingdom? It seemed like every week either the mission president or one of the zone leaders or visiting GA's was telling us that if we had real faith, we'd be baptizing. That only allowed for one conclusion.

It wasn't as if Eliza R. Snow hadn't made herself available to both Joseph Smith and Brigham Young back in the day. And I played her hymns faithfully every week.

"What do I have to do?" I asked, spreading my legs slightly. The action caught the stake president's eye, so I spread them a little wider. Something had told me when I was making the appointment he was the man I was supposed to see tonight.

Was that inspiration?

President Blake smiled and walked over to me, placing his hand on my shoulder. After he finished with me, his two counselors came into the office, one at a time. I left with three hundred dollars and an appointment to see them all again the following week. I wondered if this was the reason the Church usually only called successful businessmen to these positions. They were the only ones capable of handling the pressure.

I wondered if the money was theirs or came from tithing funds. And if the distinction mattered.

Sister Adams and I drove home in silence. I was wondering whether to donate the money I'd received to the temple fund. The more temples built, the more baptisms for the dead which could be performed, the more endowments and sealings. If I couldn't find any live converts, the spirits of the dead were just as real, just as valuable. I could certainly bring those folks to God.

It was too bad Elder Crandall wasn't in a position to help me direct money to the construction of new temples. Even if he probably needed to release as much stress for not baptizing as I did.

No, I'd better stick to mature men, I thought. Mature professionals. It was safer.

I realized I should probably feel bad about what I'd done, but I just couldn't muster any guilt. I *had* promised to consecrate everything, after all, and who else would it be but my leaders who would ask me to live up to my vows?

"Where are we going, Sister Walker?"

I turned to look at my companion, who was staring at me with a concerned expression. I seemed to be gripping the steering wheel awfully tightly. I smiled and loosened my grip.

"Just one little stop before we go home," I said. A few minutes later, we pulled up outside of Sister Garcia's apartment. I told Sister Adams to wait in the car, and I walked up to the door.

Sister Garcia opened it a moment later, her hair disheveled, weariness in every line of her face. I put the bills in her hand and gave her a quick hug. She looked at me in astonishment, and I put a finger to my lips. She nodded, and I turned around and walked back to my companion.

A Hostage for the Lord

"This is a stick up! Everybody on the floor!"

I looked up to see two men wearing ski masks pointing guns at other people in the bank. I couldn't tell if they were aiming shotguns or rifles or what. They were just big, scary guns. I dropped to my knees and pulled Sister Nesbitt down with me.

"Oh, my heck!" I whispered. "Oh, my heck!"

"Don't worry, Sister Adams," my companion whispered back. "Everything's going to be fine." Her face was expressionless.

"Oh, my heck! Oh, my heck!"

I wanted to keep my face pointing toward the floor, afraid if the bank robbers thought I might be able to describe their clothing or their height or whatever to police, they'd shoot me, but I was also afraid of them coming up behind me without me knowing, so I peeked upward. It turned out I'd missed a third bank robber. He jumped over the counter and pushed a teller toward the vault.

I turned my head to look toward the front door. It was too far to try to make a run for it. And one of the robbers was forcing the security guard to lock it. I could see the top of Smith Tower pointing up out of Pioneer Square through one corner of the glass.

"Sister Adams, everything's going to be all right." She didn't look concerned at all.

Sister Nesbitt's calm voice helped me back down out of my panic, and I started breathing more regularly. I could hear a couple of other bank customers nearby crying softly. There was a pool of water showing that one man near us had urinated on himself.

Soon, I could hear sirens, and before long, police were at the door, tugging pointlessly at the handles. A moment later, the phone rang, and one of the robbers picked it up. I couldn't hear what he said, and I couldn't see the expression on his face, given the mask, but it was clear this wasn't a good development.

Soon, I could see that the robbers had amassed five large bags filled with currency. The phone rang again, and the same man answered. After he hung up, he fired a shot into the air.

"All right, people, listen up! The police are going to give us a ride to the airport, where they're going to give us a pilot and a small plane. We'll be taking a couple of you with us, but we'll let you go when we land safely."

I felt my heartbeat getting faster again and started to hyperventilate.

"It's going to be okay, Sister Adams." Sister Nesbitt reached over and grabbed my hand. Her voice sounded hollow. I started to cry.

"I don't want to die."

She smiled slightly. "You're going to be just fine. The Lord protects his own."

"The way he protected Sister Matthews?" I asked. I was sorry as soon as I said it. How could Heavenly Father possibly help someone with such a lack of faith?

"Shut the fuck up!" One of the robbers walking nearby kicked me in the thigh. I put my fist in my mouth and felt Sister Nesbitt squeeze my hand.

Watching the robber move away, I thought about all the pain poor Sister Matthews must have endured. She was one of our investigators who we'd finally managed to baptize, despite her husband's objections. He attacked her after she came home with wet hair and he figured out where she'd been.

The man had already beaten her several times before, but this time, he went absolutely crazy. He destroyed her cell phone, and while he was distracted for a second with that task, Sister Matthews locked herself in the bathroom and crawled out the window, running to the neighbor's house to call the police.

What use were the police?

What I needed was to feel Heavenly Father's presence, know he was with me, but I didn't feel anything right now. I looked over at Sister Nesbitt, who was tracking the head bank robber with her eyes.

She'd taken the incident with Sister Matthews even harder than I had. She'd stopped participating in companionship prayer. She stopped reading her scriptures.

She even almost stopped eating, losing five pounds over the next couple of weeks. We certainly hadn't done any more missionary work. I refrained from telling the mission president out of respect. I didn't want to get her in trouble. I was sure she'd snap out of it sooner or later. Maybe the robbery was Heavenly Father's way of reaching out to her. Maybe it was his way of reaching us both.

A half hour passed. Then an hour. I was beginning to envy the man who had relieved himself. My bladder was killing me. I saw one man whispering to a man near him, and another man whispering to someone I thought might be his wife.

I was afraid one elderly woman had died of a heart attack, but then I heard her snort in her sleep. A woman a few yards away had pulled out a Sudoku book and was filling in numbers while she lay on her stomach.

What was the matter with everyone?

I felt a sudden urge to sing "I Am a Child of God." That would show Heavenly Father I had faith.

One of the men grabbed the phone and made a call. After a brief exchange I couldn't quite hear, he slammed the phone down and walked over to one of the men lying on the floor, the one who'd been whispering to his wife. He pointed downward and fired. Everyone screamed.

The phone rang a few seconds later, and the bank robber shouted into it. "I want our ride *now* or another hostage gets it every thirty minutes!"

I started crying. This time, Sister Nesbitt didn't try to comfort me.

I thought again about Sister Matthews. The police arrested her husband and put him in jail, but they told her they could only keep him forty-eight hours. Her sister offered to buy her a plane ticket anywhere she wanted to go to get away from Seattle. Sister Matthews didn't even tell us the destination. She did call the bishop and ask if he could organize the Elders Quorum to help put her things in storage.

He told her, "I'm afraid not, Sister Matthews. It might be a liability for the Church."

Sister Matthews repeated that line to us five times during our phone call, crying so hard she kept choking. Sister Nesbitt and I helped her at least move her photos and other personal items before she caught a cab to the airport.

I hoped the bank robbers weren't going to the same place she had.

About ten minutes after the first execution, my crying slowed down to a sniffle. I saw a heavily pregnant Filipina with her hands clasped in front of her, her eyes closed, her lips moving silently. The elderly woman who'd been dozing earlier was twisting her wedding ring over and over. No one was playing Sudoku now. Sister Nesbitt turned to me. "The Church keeps hostages, too," she said simply.

I frowned. Was she losing it? Maybe I had to be the strong one. Sister Nesbitt was the one who caught the spiders in our apartment and brought them outside. She was the one who argued with the store manager if the item we were buying didn't ring up at the correct price. She was the one who changed the oil in the car to save a few dollars.

But I needed to step up to the plate this time, find the faith I needed to get us both through. I heard footsteps and looked up. The head bank robber was walking slowly among all the customers lying on the floor, pausing over some of them and then walking on again. "What are you talking about?" I whispered back.

"I want to go home," she said, "but I can't. My family would be so disappointed."

"That's not the same thing."

"What about my aunt?" she returned.

"What about her?" Sister Nesbitt had never even mentioned an aunt before.

"She has a glass of wine with dinner every now and then. So when my cousin got married in the temple, she wasn't allowed to be there."

"That's not—"

We stopped talking when one of the robbers walked too close to us. After he moved off a bit, I looked at Sister Nesbitt and shook my head. There was no need to push our luck.

"We're all trapped," she said, despite my scowl, "doing whatever we're told to do, or we can't be with our families for important occasions now, or for eternity for *any* occasion."

"But…"

"We're banned from their presence if we ever step out of line."

I didn't understand where she was going with this. "Heavenly Father gives us commandments to make us happy," I whispered.

"My uncle finally divorced my aunt because she stopped going to church."

Sister Nesbitt's face looked so blank, almost if she'd had a mini-stroke from the stress and lost control of her facial muscles. I had to say something to snap her out of this. "I'm sure there were plenty of other problems in that relationship already."

Sister Nesbitt didn't reply.

The minutes ticked by. There were a couple more phone calls, more shouting, more threats, and then the head bank robber started walking among the customers again. He stopped near another man.

"Please," the man said, raising a hand to shield his head. The man he'd been whispering to earlier was holding the man's other hand. "Please."

The gunman fired. Everyone screamed again. Then the phone rang.

I started crying.

"Sister Matthews's sister called me the other day," Sister Nesbitt said.

"Stop talking," I whispered. "Stop talking."

"Her brother-in-law went over and beat *her* up until she told him where Sister Matthews had gone."

"Please stop talking."

"But she lied. And as soon as he was out the door, she called the police."

"And they arrested him! See, it *does* all work out!"

Sister Nesbitt stared up at the ceiling lights. "She lost the sight in one of her eyes," she said. "Her husband left her and took their child. He was too afraid *they'd* be hurt. He left her on her own."

"But…but…they're not Mormon," I sputtered. "You can't expect non-members to behave the right way all the time. That's why we teach them."

"I called Bishop Wright and asked for help." She didn't go on, and she didn't have to. But it wasn't fair to blame the bishop for not helping a non-member. He had to devote his time and energy to the congregation, not to random strangers.

He had to make sure enough people volunteered at the Bishop's Storehouse to give food to the poorer members. He spent hours every week doing marriage counseling. He had to make sure the Primary teachers showed up on Sunday.

"Do you know what the bishop said?" she asked.

Don't tell me, I thought, don't tell me, don't tell me.

"He told me if I really wanted to save people, I should do a better job as a missionary."

I thought back to the mission-wide conference we'd had three months ago, where a visiting Seventy called us to repentance, saying if we had faith the size of a mustard seed, we'd all be baptizing thirty people a month. When one of the elders actually did that a couple of months later, we knew it was true.

I *wanted* to be faithful. I tried. But I still wasn't baptizing. I'd hoped to be able to bring some of Sister Matthews's friends and family into the gospel, but…

I wondered if we should stand up and preach to everyone here, if maybe that was the whole reason we'd been led to come to the bank today. I wondered if we should call the robbers to repentance.

I lay on the floor, smelling the man near me lying in a puddle of urine.

"Okay, everybody, listen up!" the head bank robber shouted. "It's time. We've got our ride to the airport, with a plane waiting."

Where could they go but Canada, I thought, and didn't Canada have an extradition agreement?

The man walked slowly among the customers and stopped by the side of the pregnant woman. "Get up!" he shouted.

"Please!" the woman begged. "Please, I'm going to have a baby."

"Get up!"

Sister Nesbitt scrambled to her feet. "Take me," she said calmly. "I'm a Mormon missionary. You'll get a lot more traction out of that."

Oh, my heck! Oh, my heck! Oh, my heck!

The bank robber walked over and grabbed her arm roughly. Then he motioned for one of the other robbers to grab the pregnant woman. "She's not even pretty," Sister Nesbitt said. "And she's Filipino. No one is going to care about her. Just take me. I'm pretty. I'll be enough."

I needed to have faith, I told myself. If I had faith, I could get us all out of this. I needed to have faith. I needed to have faith.

The man looked at her, but I couldn't see his expression because of the ski mask. Finally, he motioned for his men to gather the bags of money, and they all headed to the front door, a pistol now at Sister Nesbitt's head.

She turned to look back at me, and I *knew*. I could see it in her eyes. Once they were all outside, the security guard quickly relocked the doors.

I watched as Sister Nesbitt broke away, and I heard the shot that felled her, a second before the barrage of gunfire that brought down the robbers.

Everyone screamed.

Books by Johnny Townsend

Thanks for reading! If you enjoyed this book, could you please take a few minutes to write a review online? Reviews are helpful both to me as an author and to other readers, so we'd all sincerely appreciate your writing one! And if you did enjoy the book, here are some others I've written you might want to look up:

Mormon Underwear

Zombies for Jesus

A Gay Mormon Missionary in Pompeii

The Golem of Rabbi Loew

Marginal Mormons

Gay Gaslighting

Mormon Misfits

Going-Out-Of-Religion Sale

Escape from Zion

Gayrabian Nights

Invasion of the Spirit Snatchers

Sexual Solidarity

The Washing of Brains

Sins of the Saints

The Last Days Linger

The Mysterious Madness of Mormons

Human Compassion for Beginners

Out of the Missionary's Closet

Breaking the Promise of the Promised Land

Am I My Planet's Keeper?

Have Your Cum and Eat It, Too

Strangers with Benefits

Constructing Equity

Wake Up and Smell the Missionaries

Racism by Proxy

Orgy at the STD Clinic

Please Evacuate

Recommended Daily Humanity

The Camper Killings

An Eternity of Mirrors: Best Short Stories of Johnny Townsend

Kinky Quilts: Patchwork Designs for Gay Men

Inferno in the French Quarter: The UpStairs Lounge Fire

Latter-Gay Saints: An Anthology of Gay Mormon Fiction (co-editor)

Available from your favorite online or neighborhood bookstore.

Wondering what some of those other books are about? Read on!

Invasion of the Spirit Snatchers

During the Apocalypse, a group of Mormon survivors in Hurricane, Utah gather in the home of the Relief Society president, telling stories to pass the time as they ration their food storage and await the Second Coming. But this is no ordinary group of Mormons—or perhaps it is. They are the faithful, feminist, gay, apostate, and repentant, all working together to help each other through the darkest days any of them have yet seen.

Gayrabian Nights

Gayrabian Nights is a twist on the well-known classic, *1001 Arabian Nights*, in which Scheherazade, under the threat of death if she ceases to captivate King Shahryar's attention, enchants him through a series of mysterious, adventurous, and romantic tales.

In this variation, a male escort, invited to the hotel room of a closeted, homophobic Mormon senator, learns that the man is poised to vote on a piece of anti-gay legislation the following morning. To prevent him from sleeping, so that the exhausted senator will miss casting his vote on the Senate floor, the escort entertains him with stories of homophobia, celibacy, mixed orientation marriages, reparative therapy, coming out, first love, gay marriage, and long-term successful gay relationships.

The escort crafts the stories to give the senator a crash course in gay culture and sensibilities, hoping to bring the man closer to accepting his own sexual orientation.

Inferno in the French Quarter: The UpStairs Lounge Fire

On Gay Pride Day in 1973, someone set the entrance to a French Quarter gay bar on fire. In the terrible inferno that followed, thirty-two people lost their lives, including a third of the local congregation of the Metropolitan Community Church, their pastor burning to death halfway out a second-story window as he tried to claw his way to freedom.

A mother who'd gone to the bar with her two gay sons died alongside them. A man who'd helped his friend escape first was found dead near the fire escape. Two children waited outside a movie theater across town for a father and "uncle" who would never pick them up. During this era of rampant homophobia, several families refused to claim the bodies, and many churches refused to bury the dead.

Author Johnny Townsend pored through old records and tracked down survivors of the fire as well as relatives and friends of those killed to compile this fascinating account of a forgotten moment in gay history.

A Gay Mormon Missionary in Pompeii

What is a gay Mormon missionary doing in Italy? He is trying to save his own soul as well as the souls of others. In these tales chronicling the two-year mission of Robert Anderson, we see a young man tormented by his inability to be the man the Church says he should be. In addition to his personal hell, Anderson faces a major earthquake, organized crime, a serious bus accident, and much more. He copes with horrendous mission leaders and his own suicidal tendencies. But one day, he meets another missionary who loves him, and his world changes forever.

The Golem of Rabbi Loew

Jacob and Esau Cohen are the closest of brothers. In fact, they're lovers. A doctor tries to combine canine genes with those of Jews, to improve their chances of surviving a hostile world. A Talmudic scholar dates an escort. A scientist tries to develop the "God spot" in the brains of his patients in hopes of creating a messiah.

A Jew-by-Choice navigates Jewish/Muslim relations during Pesach. A gay Lubavitcher dating a Catholic is attacked and left for dead but becomes a police officer in response. The Golem of Prague is really Rabbi Loew's secret lover.

While some of the Jews in Townsend's book are Orthodox, this collection of Jewish stories most certainly is not.

Am I My Planet's Keeper?

Global Warming. Climate Change. Climate Crisis. Climate Emergency. Whatever label we use, we are facing one of the greatest challenges to the survival of life as we know it.

But while addressing greenhouse gases is perhaps our most urgent need, it's not our only task. We must also address toxic waste, pollution, habitat destruction, and our other contributions to the world's sixth mass extinction event.

In order to do that, we must simultaneously address the unmet human needs that keep us distracted from deeper engagement in stabilizing our climate: moderating economic inequality, guaranteeing healthcare to all, and ensuring education for everyone.

And to accomplish *that*, we must unite to combat the monied forces that use fear, prejudice, and misinformation to manipulate us.

It's a daunting task. But success is our only option.

Wake Up and Smell the Missionaries

Two Mormon missionaries in Italy discover they share the same rare ability—both can emit pheromones on demand. At first, they playfully compete in the hills of Frascati to see who can tempt "investigators" most. But soon they're targeting each other non-stop.

Can two immature young men learn to control their "superpower" to live a normal life…and develop genuine love? Even as their relationship is threatened by the attentions of another man?

They seem just on the verge of success when a massive earthquake leaves them trapped under the rubble of their apartment in Castellammare.

With night falling and temperatures dropping, can they dig themselves out in time to save themselves? And will their injuries destroy the ability that brought them together in the first place?

Orgy at the STD Clinic

Todd Tillotson is struggling to move on after his husband is killed in a hit and run attack a year earlier during a Black Lives Matter protest in Seattle.

In this novel set entirely on public transportation, we watch as Todd, isolated throughout the pandemic, battles desperation in his attempt to safely reconnect with the world.

Will he find love again, even casual friendship, or will he simply end up another crazy old man on the bus?

Things don't look good until a man whose face he can't even see sits down beside him despite the raging variants.

And asks him a question that will change his life.

Please Evacuate

A gay, partygoing New Yorker unconcerned about the future or the unsustainability of capitalism is hit by a truck and thrust into a straight man's body half a continent away. As Hunter tries to figure out what's happening, he's caught up in another disaster, a wildfire sweeping through a

Colorado community, the flames overtaking him and several schoolchildren as they flee.

When he awakens, Hunter finds himself in the body of yet another man, this time in northern Italy, a former missionary about to marry a young Mormon woman. Still piecing together this new reality, and beginning to embrace his latest identity, Hunter fights for his life in a devastating flash flood along with his wife *and* his new husband.

He's an aging worker in drought-stricken Texas, a nurse at an assisted living facility in the direct path of a hurricane, an advocate for the unhoused during a freak Seattle blizzard.

We watch as Hunter is plunged into life after life, finally recognizing the futility of only looking out for #1 and understanding the part he must play in addressing the global climate crisis…if he ever gets another chance.

Recommended Daily Humanity

A checklist of human rights must include basic housing, universal healthcare, equitable funding for public schools, and tuition-free college and vocational training.

In addition to the basics, though, we need much more to fully thrive. Subsidized childcare, universal pre-K, a universal basic income, subsidized high-speed internet, net neutrality, fare-free public transit (plus *more* public transit), and medically assisted death for the terminally ill who want it.

None of this will matter, though, if we neglect to address the rapidly worsening climate crisis.

Sound expensive? It is.

But not as expensive as refusing to implement these changes. The cost of climate disasters each year has grown to staggering figures. And the cost of social and political upheaval from not meeting the needs of suffering workers, families, and individuals may surpass even that.

It's best we understand that the vast sums required to enact meaningful change are an investment which will pay off not only in some indeterminate future but in fact almost immediately. And without these adjustments to our lifestyles and values, there may very well not be a future capable of sustaining freedom and democracy…or even civilization itself.

The Camper Killings

When a homeless man is found murdered a few blocks from Morgan Beylerian's house in south Seattle, everyone seems to consider the body just so much additional trash to be cleared from the neighborhood. But Morgan liked the guy. They used to chat when Morgan brought Nick groceries once a week.

And the brutal way the man was killed reminds Morgan of their shared Mormon heritage, back when the faithful agreed to have their throats slit if they ever revealed temple secrets.

Did Nick's former wife take action when her ex-husband refused to grant a temple divorce? Did his murder have something to do with the public accusations that brought an end to his promising career?

Morgan does his best to investigate when no one else seems to care, but it isn't easy as a man living paycheck to paycheck himself, only able to pursue his investigation via public transit.

As he continues his search for the killer, Morgan's friends withdraw and his husband threatens to leave. When another homeless man is killed and Morgan is accused of the crime, things look even bleaker.

But his troubles aren't over yet.

Will Morgan find the killer before the killer finds him?

What Readers Have Said

Townsend's stories are "a gay *Portnoy's Complaint* of Mormonism. Salacious, sweet, sad, insightful, insulting, religiously ethnic, quirky-faithful, and funny."

D. Michael Quinn, author of *The Mormon Hierarchy: Origins of Power*

"Told from a believably conversational first-person perspective, [*A Gay Mormon Missionary in Pompeii*'s] novelistic focus on Anderson's journey to thoughtful self-acceptance allows for greater character development than often seen in short stories, which makes this well-paced work rich and satisfying, and one of Townsend's strongest. An extremely important contribution to the field of Mormon fiction." Named to Kirkus Reviews' Best of 2011.

Kirkus Reviews

"The thirteen stories in *Mormon Underwear* capture this struggle [between Mormonism and homosexuality] with humor, sadness, insight, and sometimes shocking details....*Mormon Underwear* provides compelling stories, literally from the inside-out."

Niki D'Andrea, *Phoenix New Times*

"Townsend's lively writing style and engaging characters [in *Zombies for Jesus*] make for stories which force us to wake up, smell the (prohibited) coffee, and review our attitudes with regard to reading dogma so doggedly. These are tales which revel in the individual tics and quirks which make us human, Mormon or not, gay or not…"

A.J. Kirby, *The Short Review*

"The Rift," from *A Gay Mormon Missionary in Pompeii*, is a "fascinating tale of an untenable situation…a *tour de force*."

David Lenson, editor, *The Massachusetts Review*

"Pronouncing the Apostrophe," from *The Golem of Rabbi Loew*, is "quiet and revealing, an intriguing tale…"

Sima Rabinowitz, Literary Magazine Review, *NewPages.com*

The Circumcision of God is "a collection of short stories that consider the imperfect, silenced majority of Mormons, who may in fact be [the Church's] best hope….[The book leaves] readers regretting the church's willingness to marginalize those who best exemplify its ideals: those who love fiercely despite all obstacles, who brave challenges at great personal risk and who always choose the hard, higher road."

Kirkus Reviews

In *Mormon Fairy Tales*, Johnny Townsend displays "both a wicked sense of irony and a deep well of compassion."

Kel Munger, *Sacramento News and Review*

Zombies for Jesus is "eerie, erotic, and magical."

Publishers Weekly

"While [Townsend's] many touching vignettes draw deeply from Mormon mythology, history, spirituality and culture, [*Mormon Fairy Tales*] is neither a gaudy act of proselytism nor angry protest literature from an ex-believer. Like all good fiction, his stories are simply about the joys, the hopes and the sorrows of people."

Kirkus Reviews

"In *Inferno in the French Quarter* author Johnny Townsend restores this tragic event [the UpStairs Lounge fire] to its proper place in LGBT history and reminds us that the victims of the blaze were not just 'statistics,' but real people with real lives, families, and friends."

Jesse Monteagudo, *The Bilerico Project*

In *Inferno in the French Quarter*, "Townsend's heart-rending descriptions of the victims…seem to [make them] come alive once more."

Kit Van Cleave, *OutSmart Magazine*

Marginal Mormons is "an irreverent, honest look at life outside the mainstream Mormon Church….Throughout his musings on sin and forgiveness, Townsend beautifully demonstrates his characters' internal, perhaps irreconcilable struggles….Rather than anger and disdain, he offers an honest portrayal of people searching for meaning and community in their lives, regardless of their life choices or secrets." Named to Kirkus Reviews' Best of 2012.

Kirkus Reviews

The stories in *The Mormon Victorian Society* "register the new openness and confidence of gay life in the age of same-sex marriage….What hasn't changed is Townsend's wry, conversational prose, his subtle evocations of character and social dynamics, and his deadpan humor. His warm empathy still glows in this intimate yet clear-eyed engagement with Mormon theology and folkways. Funny, shrewd and finely wrought dissections of the awkward contradictions—and surprising harmonies—between conscience and desire." Named to Kirkus Reviews' Best of 2013.

Kirkus Reviews

"This collection of short stories [*The Mormon Victorian Society*] featuring gay Mormon characters slammed [me] in the face from the first page, wrestled my heart and mind to the floor, and left me panting and wanting more by the end. Johnny Townsend has created so many memorable characters in such few pages. I went weeks thinking about this book. It truly touched me."

Tom Webb, *A Bear on Books*

Dragons of the Book of Mormon is an "entertaining collection....Townsend's prose is sharp, clear, and easy to read, and his characters are well rendered..."

Publishers Weekly

"The pre-eminent documenter of alternative Mormon lifestyles...Townsend has a deep understanding of his characters, and his limpid prose, dry humor and well-grounded (occasionally magical) realism make their spiritual conundrums both compelling and entertaining. [*Dragons of the Book of Mormon* is] [a]nother of Townsend's critical but affectionate and absorbing tours of Mormon discontent." Named to Kirkus Reviews' Best of 2014.

Kirkus Reviews

In *Gayrabian Nights*, "Townsend's prose is always limpid and evocative, and…he finds real drama and emotional depth in the most ordinary of lives."

Kirkus Reviews

Gayrabian Nights is a "complex revelation of how seriously soul damaging the denial of the true self can be."

Ryan Rhodes, author of *Free Electricity*

Gayrabian Nights "was easily the most original book I've read all year. Funny, touching, topical, and thoroughly enjoyable."

Rainbow Awards

Lying for the Lord is "one of the most gripping books that I've picked up for quite a while. I love the author's writing style, alternately cynical, humorous, biting, scathing, poignant, and touching…. This is the third book of his that I've read, and all are equally engaging. These are stories that need to be told, and the author does it in just the right way."

Heidi Alsop, *Ex-Mormon Foundation Board Member*

In *Lying for the Lord*, Townsend "gets under the skin of his characters to reveal their complexity and conflicts....shrewd, evocative [and] wryly humorous."

Kirkus Reviews

In *Missionaries Make the Best Companions*, "the author treats the clash between religious dogma and liberal humanism with vivid realism, sly humor, and subtle feeling as his characters try to figure out their true missions in life. Another of Townsend's rich dissections of Mormon failures and uncertainties..." Named to Kirkus Reviews' Best of 2015.

Kirkus Reviews

In *Invasion of the Spirit Snatchers*, "Townsend, a confident and practiced storyteller, skewers the hypocrisies and eccentricities of his characters with precision and affection. The outlandish framing narrative is the most consistent source of shock and humor, but the stories do much to ground the reader in the world—or former world—of the characters....A funny, charming tale about a group of Mormons facing the end of the world."

Kirkus Reviews

"Townsend's collection [*The Washing of Brains*] once again displays his limpid, naturalistic prose, skillful narrative chops, and his subtle insights into psychology...Well-crafted dispatches on the clash between religion and self-fulfillment..."

Kirkus Reviews

"While the author is generally at his best when working as a satirist, there are some fine, understated touches in these tales [*The Last Days Linger*] that will likely affect readers in subtle ways….readers should come away impressed by the deep empathy he shows for all his characters—even the homophobic ones."

Kirkus Reviews

"Written in a conversational style that often uses stories and personal anecdotes to reveal larger truths, this immensely approachable book [*Racism by Proxy*] skillfully serves its intended audience of White readers grappling with complex questions regarding race, history, and identity. The author's frequent references to the Church of Jesus Christ of Latter-day Saints may be too niche for readers unfamiliar with its idiosyncrasies, but Townsend generally strikes a perfect balance of humor, introspection, and reasoned arguments that will engage even skeptical readers."

Kirkus Reviews

Orgy at the STD Clinic portrays "an all-too real scenario that Townsend skewers to wincingly accurate proportions…[with] instant classic moments courtesy of his punchy, sassy, sexy lead character…"

Jim Piechota, *Bay Area Reporter*

Orgy at the STD Clinic is "…a triumph of humane sensibility. A richly textured saga that brilliantly captures the fraying social fabric of contemporary life." Named to Kirkus Reviews' Best Indie Books of 2022.

Kirkus Reviews

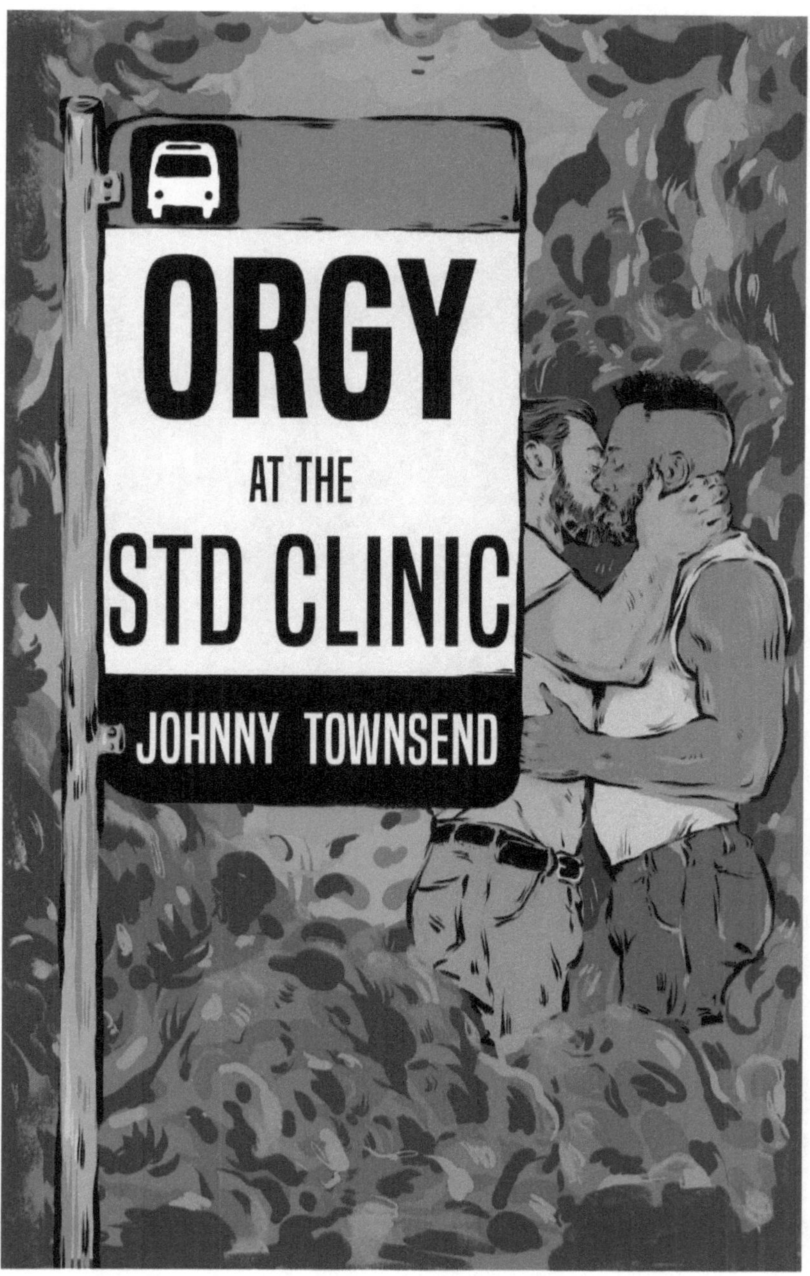

ORGY
AT THE
STD CLINIC
JOHNNY TOWNSEND

HAVE YOUR CUM AND AND EAT IT, TOO
JOHNNY TOWNSEND

Going-Out-Of-
Religion Sale
JOHNNY TOWNSEND

9 781961 525023